McCAFFERY

McCAFFERY

CHARLES GORHAM

CUTTING EDGE

ISBN-13: 978-1-962896-15-3

Published by
Cutting Edge Books
PO Box 8212
Calabasas, CA 91372
www.cuttingedgebooks.com

CHAPTER ONE

FOR five years I have been happy. Surely this is a kind of record, if one excepts the members of those religious orders who relapse into mouthless adoration, finding joy in the silent creation of wine and cheese and fragrant honey. The honey I tasted once in my mother's kitchen. *Miel de la Trappe,* pale Canadian honey, smelling of northern wild flowers. It was an extravagance never repeated. The white-robed monk on the tin had caused her to forget to ask the price, though she was usually careful with my father's money.

The white-robed monk on the tin was happy, holding the beehive in his hand, his lips sealed by the force of his devotion. He had withdrawn into God and he was happy.

But I am no Trappist. I read, not precisely at will to be sure, but in quantity and with close attention, so that Dorion assures me that I could meet the doctoral requirements in literature. I smoke cigarettes when this is permitted. I think of myself rather than of God. And I talk. For a great period after my first year here, which was a year of Trappist silence, I did, it would seem, almost nothing but talk, to myself, alone in the night, to Dorion and to those appointed to listen to me.

I am happy. I have been happy these last five years. I do not mean that I have been content or satisfied or resigned or happy as a vegetable may be happy. I have been positively happy, aware of safety, of joy in living and of self-discovery. I am often serene.

There is no violence left in me. It has vanished in the warmth of the sun.

"Soon they will ask you to leave," Dorion tells me this morning.

"But I don't want to go," I protest.

"They will persuade you," Dorion says calmly.

We are sorting books into a cart from which they will be returned to the shelves. I work in the library during the afternoons; mornings I work with my hands on the farm. The division of labor is obligatory, but I should not change it, offered the chance.

"Will they force me to go?" I ask Dorion with a vision of myself stripped naked and cast into the void of the world.

Dorion smiles, a radiant, professional smile. When he smiles he is benign. His students adored him and refused to believe even his own confessions. In his day he was a Harvard legend. Perhaps he is remembered in Cambridge now, after thirty years. He has the gift. He is a great teacher. Socrates in Bedlam.

"Of course not," he assures me. "They will not even mention the prospect of your departure. But they will see to it that you ask to leave. They will oppose you for a time. Then you will persuade them that it is time for you to go."

I shake my head.

"Oh, yes," says Dorion confidently. "I am nearly the oldest inhabitant, Vincent. I have watched the machinery for many years. You will go."

I look at him desperately. My happiness is threatened. To leave this valley with its pretty Indian name and its stunning beauty would be to risk all that I have gained. I am terrified at the thought. I drop a book, pick it up slowly. Dorion touches my shoulder.

"You should go," he says gently. "It will be possible for you to survive. I know you, Vincent. I promise you, it will be possible."

I take his hand. We are friends. There is a bond between us that bridges a gap of more than forty years. We love books and we are interested in the raising of ethical questions. We do not find answers. We do not seek answers. But for us there is a certain astringent value to be gained from raising the questions clearly and exposing them to light. I am Dorion's pupil. In a sense I am his son. There is love between us, gentle and quite pure.

Certain other things we share. We are both murderers. In this community that is not a matter of great distinction. Nevertheless it tightens the bond between us.

I release his hand. "I am frightened," I say.

"Of course," says Dorion. "But for you it is possible. I should not go myself. I am free here and out there I should be a slave. But I lived out there for forty years. You came here as a child, with the face of an altar boy. You must go back."

"Is it possible?" I ask. I am doubtful. For the first time in years I shudder at the thought of my own past.

"The things that brought you here: the acts themselves, you would not repeat them," says Dorion. "I know that."

"There would be no point," I agree.

I wheel the little cart to the shelves and begin the chore of returning the books to their places. Ordinarily I enjoy this work but now my serenity is disturbed and I make frustrating errors. I am troubled.

Inmate, I think. The word quivers in my mind like a dagger thrown into wood.

The term is no longer in fashion. The preferred word is patient. Yet inmate contains its attractions. One is In. Therefore, he is not Out. He is a Mate. Therefore he is provided with mates or companions, fellow-sharers. Dorion and I, we two murderers, forty-odd years apart in age, we are in, and out of the cold, guarded by the walls and the gates, safe from the tiger at the gates. And we are mates. We are companions, celibate, innocent lovers if you like.

To return, to pass through the gates and stand in the space that exists on the other side of the wall, is not a prospect that attracts me. I brood about it through the afternoon.

"They will move you perhaps to another institution," Dorion tells me. "Then to a minimum-security ward. Then they will give you weekend leave."

"And then I will stand on the corner of the street, alone and freezing," I say to him.

We sit in the recreation hall, a chessboard between us. Dorion moves carefully. "Your queen, Vincent," he says. "Pay attention to the game, my boy. Have I taught you for nothing?"

The great hall is silent. Suddenly a patient shrieks, then darts like a terrified deer toward the grilled window. Attendants seize him at once. They lift him as if he were a basket and carry him toward the door. He shrieks, being carried, as if the soles of his feet were burnt by live coals.

Dorion and I are not disturbed. It is as though in the outside world two taxicabs had grazed fenders. A screaming patient, carried away … it is an everyday incident for one whose home is a hospital for the criminal insane.

Of course I am not insane. Nor is Dorion. We are murderers both, criminals, but we are not insane. We are rational. And the murders had their own severe logic. They were the products of their own necessity. Perhaps this is true of all murders, even the most banal.

Three years ago as an exercise I memorized all of Euclid, in Euclid's language, every page and by heart, using a text imposed upon English schoolboys more than a century ago. (One has a great deal of time in a place like this.) In the dark air before my face as I lay in my bed at night I could call up any page I liked, see it almost precisely as Euclid must have seen it under the sensuous Alexandrine sun.

In the same way, I have geometrized the events that brought me to this place. This is a good institution. The men and women appointed here are selfless and capable. I have been helped, but I have also helped myself. I have created my own freedom within these walls and given myself the means with which to create it freshly every day.

The past is all in my mind like a film wound on a spool, to be run at whatever speed I like, backward or forward as I choose. I have mastered it all. I understand. I forgive others. I experience grief. I forgive myself. And yet I am afraid. I am stirred by agitation.

Dorion defeats me at chess. We return the board and the men to the counter, then go to the canteen, where we each buy a cup of coffee with hospital scrip.

Even here in this locked place it appears that I am a free agent obliged to make choices. Of course, I can force them to keep me here. I can scream in the way the carried patient screamed. That would be a choice. I can commit another murder. Murders have been committed here, inside the walls.

But I hold the hot cup in the palms of my hands and I know that I will do none of the things that would oblige them to keep me here. My hands are burning. The cup is made of green plastic. Unbreakable. The fierce heat of the coffee comes through the thin brittle shell. I sip the coffee, then put the cup on the table. I blow on the palms of my hands.

"If I were your age I would take the risk," Dorion says. He has a method of holding the cup so that his fingers are not burnt. Even in trifles he is experienced. He smiles at me. "Without doubt, my dear boy, I should take the risk," he says. "If I were your age."

I am twenty-three. I look at Dorion gratefully. He has shaped my mind and in doing this has held the sharp edge of his own. I am important to him. When I go, there will be an emptiness in the air around him. Yet out of love he urges me to leave this place, where he will die.

I am twenty-three. When it began I was sixteen, a few weeks away from my seventeenth birthday. It is all in my mind, ordered, unvarying, definite as the text of a Greek play processed by the hands of scholars.

The books that enter this establishment are carefully reviewed. Things that might be disturbing are barred. Yet the fifty plays of Greece are here, in a set with dark blue covers, Attic syllables on one page, English text on the other.

Oedipus at Colonus. Oedipus Rex. Oedipus of the streaming eyes. Oedipus in Yorkville on the East Side of the City of New York.

Raskolnikov has no home on the Puritan shelves of our library but I know Raskolnikov as a brother. It was Bentley who forced me to read the book, who lashed me through it. "The poor man's Raskolnikov," he called me sometimes. "The American version. Made of plastic, my dear boy, and without the Slavic interior."

Perhaps.

It is time for us to be locked away. I leave Dorion. We shake hands, as we always do in the evening, as if we were Parisians in the Bois de Boulogne. I walk through the polished corridors unattended, passing patients dressed in blouses that have been dyed a chemical green.

I must have worn the green blouse during the year when I did not speak and for some time after I began to speak. Everyone wears it when first he comes, but I cannot remember wearing it. I cannot remember being led by the arm or carried between two attendants as if I were a basket.

I am dressed in ordinary clothes, army trousers, a blue work shirt nicely faded, light-weight work shoes. I look, I suppose, like a young farmer. I have a tiny room of my own with a bed, a washstand, a chair and a table. It is the reward for good behavior, for tractability, bestowed by the State of New York as an expression of trust in the occupant. The Inmate. The protected and guarded one. The Insider. The possessor of companions.

I sit on the edge of the narrow cot in my room and take a bundle of photographs from a small box beneath the bed. There is a strip of photographs of myself, passport size or a little larger, taken in a booth at Woolworth's store on Third Avenue more than seven years ago. You enter the booth, draw the curtain, feed a quarter into the slot and pose. The machine clicks four times. In a few seconds the strip of prints emerges from the bowels of the enormous camera, dry and ready to be clipped apart, the various poses given to girls who hoard such photographs in lumpy wallets.

This strip has never been clipped apart. When the pictures were taken I had no girl to whom even one of them might be given.

I look at the face on the glossy paper, the same face four times repeated with scarcely a change in the cast of the head or the set of the lips. I had not moved in the little booth while the lights blazed into my face.

It is the face of a murderer. This is a known, an established fact. This face confessed to the murders, and so this is the face of murder.

It is also the face of innocence, and the eyes are alive with a kind of trusting wonder.

"When you came here," Dorion said, "you had the face of an altar boy."

"Why not?" I had answered. "For a long time I served Mass at St. J————'s Church in Yorkville, where I was born."

It was "Irish Yorkville," far to the east, near the river, pressed toward the river by the great wedge of Germans. In its day the neighborhood was like a village immersed in the concrete of the city, with the mores of an Irish village. All that has passed. East Yorkville is one of the New York neighborhoods that are breaking up after two and three generations of parochial continuity. People whose grandparents came from Ireland and settled in the East 80s are moving away to Queens and Brooklyn and even to the hated Protestant suburbs, some from choice, encouraged by the general change in fortune, others because one by one the old tenements are coming down to make way for luxury housing.

When I lived in East Yorkville nearly everyone was moving away or talking about it, but there were diehards who until the very end would refuse to be forced from their native heath and they were as jealous of the concrete earth as was ever a Galway peasant of his patch of wet rich soil.

My father was one of the diehards so that my mother and I, until my mother died, lived in East Yorkville though neither of us, to the eye at least, seemed in any way to belong there.

My mother.

I sit on the edge of the madhouse cot and remember my pretty mother. She was religious and romantic. It is always a dangerous combination. As I grew up, I absorbed her passion for the Church and her awe of distant and mighty places.

"You will see Rome, my child," she would whisper to me when I was young. "You will see His Holiness himself, touch his ring and kiss it. Think of it, Vincent, one day you may be a cardinal. A prince of the Church. Think of it, Vincent, a prince!"

It was her vocation, not mine, but I accepted it. Oh, yes. From the day of my birth to the day of her death I accepted it. I was to be a priest of God. It was what my mother had planned for me while she carried me in her womb. My vocation was born before I was conceived, and as long as my mother drew breath on this earth it was simply a fact, not a thing to be questioned.

I loved her. I loved her so much that in all my young life, until she died, I never loved anyone else, not my father or my aunt or a girl or a schoolmate, not anyone in all the world except my lovely, fragile mother.

She was pale and tender and of romantically delicate health. She was lovely and fair, the Rose of Tralee, and the truth as she knew it dawned in her eyes. I was strangled in life for the love of my mother, yet I cannot find the heart to blame her. I sit on the edge of my narrow bed and weep a little for her now.

I looked again at the face on the film strip. I recognize it as my own face, yet it is not mine. I look at the reflection of my own face in the steel mirror that is bolted to the wall. I see the face of a young man, black-haired, blue-eyed, a face that is physically related to the photographed face, but physically only.

I look at the photographs again. I see the face of a handsome boy, with which face it is impossible to associate the idea of any crime whatsoever. It is the face of a boy who might be expected, without priggishness or affectation, to say "sir" to his elders or to give up his seat on the bus to a lady.

It is my face, yet it is not mine.

It is the face of Vincent Michael Joseph McCaffery, victim and murderer, and chief character in the Greek play that has been formed in my mind during these years that I have lived among the gentle and the violent mad.

Oedipus Rex. Oedipus in Yorkville.

I undress, switch off the light, get into bed, and switch on the magic lantern that is in my mind. All around me the madhouse sleeps. Armed guards pace the outer walls as guards paced the walls of windy Troy. I lay safe in my narrow bed running the film through my mind again.

CHAPTER TWO

GO straight back in time to the night of the crap game that summer, when I lost all my money.

We were in an alley behind the Yorkville Gem. I can feel the heat of the summer night and my ears adjust themselves to the familiar neighborhood accent, an accent that was partly mine.

Beano Malloy had the dice. He rubbed them between his palms, blew on them once and shot. As he shot somebody yelled: "Make them dice bounce, Beano. Make 'em bounce off the wall." It was an open-air game in what had once been the stage-door alley. A forty-watt bulb in a wire cage high above us shed a feeble light. You could just make out the white dice as they left Beano's hand and struck the brick of the alley wall. They bounced all right. It was dark enough so that Beano might have tried to use a loaded pair but Beano was too smart for that. Too smart and too lucky. A flashlight came on for an instant, showing the dice and the money in the pot—ten dollars' worth of bills and silver. The dice showed a four and a three. It was Beano's fourth straight pass. He showed no reaction at all, just rattled the dice in his hand and said dead-pan, "Let it ride, suckers. Let it ride again."

His small, predacious face was relentless. His Irish eyes were like bits of shrapnel. He was invulnerable. I had been kneeling beside the pot. Now I stood up, brushing off the knees of my pants. Conny Donovan was beside me.

"That does it," I said. "The boy wonder has cleaned me out."

"Me too," Conny said. "Is he crooked or just lucky?"

The others laughed. Beano ignored Conny, drawing down half of what was in the pot, still trying to get faded, rattling the bones gently in his hand. He was fifteen and small for his age, was Beano, but already he was a businessman when it came to gambling, sharp and merciless in these street games as if he were a big-time operator standing behind a green baize table.

Conny and I drifted out of the alley, checking first to make sure there wasn't a squad car in sight. Sometimes when they were bored the police cruised through the streets, breaking up these neighborhood games and chasing people from the street corners.

There were no police. Side by side we walked east, companions in penury if nothing else. I had known Conny all my life but he was an acquaintance, not a friend. I had no friends and my mother had been my only confidante.

It was morbidly hot, a sultry night. All around us the city lay, vanquished in a swamp of heat. Dressed in a T shirt and chino trousers, still I felt the heat. It was the first week in July and the monstrous metropolitan summer was before us, weeks of it, months of it, when the only respite from the heat would be found in an air-cooled movie house or on the beach at Coney Island.

The summers here in the mountains where the madhouse stands are cool and sweet. To work on the farm under the upstate sun is pleasant. During the day or in the pale mountain evenings I can scarcely remember the misery of a New York summer. But as I lie on the madhouse cot, the film of my memory whipping past, the sense of recall is sharp and total. I feel the sweat on my flesh and the stench of the city is in my nostrils. Here where I am safe, where the strangers are locked out and armed guards bar one's enemies, I can feel the heat of the city summer and sense the contagious evil of the city's streets.

Other summers I had gone away to Murphy's Farm in the Catskills, with my mother, or, when I was older, to the Action

Camp for Catholic Youth in the low hills of New Jersey. In that summer, my seventeenth, my mother was ten months dead and buried under a polished granite stone and I was too old for the Catholic camp.

"So it is Tuesday and we're both broke," I said. "What do we do now?"

On the street corners of Yorkville money or the lack of it automatically supplied itself as a topic for conversation.

Conny shrugged. "I don't know," he said. "Last week my old man gave me a fin, but with it he gave me a lecture as if it was his last five bucks or maybe the last five bucks in the world."

"I could get some money from my aunt," I said. "Except that she's on her vacation and won't be back for ten days. My old man won't give me a nickel until Saturday. He believes in discipline."

"Go to work, says my old man," Conny told me. "Get off your ass and go to work."

"At what?" I said.

It was a bad summer for teen-age jobs. There were articles in the newspapers about it. I clipped one out and pasted it to a piece of cardboard, intending to show it to my father if he brought up the question of a summer job. He did not raise the issue but he was firm about the allowance.

We were too old for camp and too young to get jobs that summer. At least no one had offered us jobs that we would take. The good jobs, in offices, went to boys over seventeen. What we could get were what the neighborhood called slob jobs: messenger boy, delivery boy, paper route at five in the morning. Lousy jobs, lousy pay. We were arrogant Irish-Americans, filled with a fierce sense of caste. We left those jobs to the colored boys or the Puerto Rican kids who had to work if they wanted to eat.

We did nothing that summer. In Donovan's phrase, we "hanged around."

Mostly we hanged around the neighborhood, playing ball in the street, shooting craps in the alley, standing endlessly on various corners watching the girls as they passed by. We pretended to enjoy doing nothing and most of the time it wasn't so bad.

If you had money.

In camp there was always something to do. Every day we went swimming. We played volleyball and baseball and there were boxing and wrestling matches. In the mess hall every evening there was a moving-picture show. Everything was free. A dollar a week was all you could spend, for Cokes and maybe a package of cigarettes. In camp, being broke didn't matter.

But hanging around East Yorkville broke was worse than being in jail, worse than being locked up in the Kips Bay Psychiatric Hospital, which, on that hot summer's night, was the closest I had been to being in jail.

You have to have money in the city.

Without money you can do nothing but hold up a brick wall and watch the girls go by, which is what we were doing that night, Conny Donovan and I.

It was Tuesday night. On Saturday night my father would hand me five one-dollar bills, my allowance; that was supposed to last me until the next Saturday night. He thought it was a lot of money when he handed it to me. When he was passing it across the bar at Mallin's or Murphy's it was nothing.

"When I was your age I was swinging a hoe," he would tell me, marveling at my good fortune as he handed me the money. "Mixing mortar and carrying brick, that was me at fifteen. And I didn't get no five dollars for myself. A dollar on Saturday night, that's what I got, after a week of man's work."

I never argued with him. I took the money, thanked him and put it into my pocket, thinking, He can afford it. He earned a hundred and sixty dollars a week, even when he only worked his forty hours. With overtime some weeks he would top two hundred. Sometimes he had counted his money in front of my mother and me, tossing the dirty bills onto the parlor floor. "Two hundred and ten," he would say. "Not bad for a week's work for a man that hardly went to school." He could afford the five dollars he gave me on Saturday night and he could afford the five hundred a year that he paid for school. I took the money, but I hated to take it because it came from him. Perhaps that is why I had lost it all to predatory Beano Malloy.

On the film of my memory the old bitterness rises, acid as death in my mouth. I am free of it now in the daytime and mostly in the nighttime too, but I feel it when I call up the past, as I do in this instant.

We stood on the corner, Conny and I, watching the people pass by, well-dressed people from Gracie Square with money in their pockets, all of them going somewhere, to the show or to eat in a first-class restaurant or to drink whisky in a rich bar or to commit fornication in a wide, expensive bed.

"For-r-r-nication," I said aloud, using the calcified accent of the priest who had preached the young men's mission, warning us all against various evils.

Two girls marched toward us wearing Bermuda shorts and socks, young kids about our age. Conny straightened up. The half-light obscured his acne. The girls cast an eye in our direction. Conny nudged me with his elbow.

"What's the use?" I said. "That's elevator-house stuff, kid. We can't even buy them a lousy Coke. With them you would need operating dough, even if it was only fifteen cents."

The fragrant, untouchable girls passed by.

"Yeah, you're right," Conny agreed, leaning against the wall again. "Jesus, Mary and frigging Joseph. Tuesday. Four days until your old man springs. Five until mine comes across. Whadda we gonna do with the time?"

"Maybe we can put the arm on one of the fellows," I said, not really being serious. I was less troubled than Conny by the prospect of being broke for a week. I could read, for one thing. And sometimes I was satisfied to be alone. Conny read nothing and he was gregarious as an ant. For him the outlook was grim.

"Put the arm on Beano Malloy? Don't be simple, man," he said. "Beano would want ten per cent interest if he loaned you the sweat off his backside. As for money, he wouldn't loan a dime to his own mother, and the way that crap game was going Beano must have all the money in Yorkville by now."

A wave of depression swept over me. What am I doing here? I thought. None of this really concerned me. I was here on the corner with Conny, pretending to be a neighborhood kid, impersonating a street-corner boy. I was not a neighborhood boy, although I had been born in Yorkville and passed all of my life in the neighborhood. I had been marked off at birth, cut off from the others, so that while they accepted me I was like the token Jew taken into a Christian club, a member but never quite a member, a member who remains an outsider. I could speak in the neighborhood cadences when I was on the street corner. They were not the cadences of my thoughts. Another thing cut me off from the boys who had grown up around me. I went neither to the public school nor to the parochial high school but to an institution that was private and military and overlooked by Jesuits, a school that my mother had selected and that stood, monolithic and soot-covered, several miles from Yorkville, in lower Manhattan, a granite fortress of a school squatting behind the carved letters: A.M.D.G.

Ad majorem Dei gloriam.

All my life in that neighborhood I had been the insider-outsider, never quite a member of the lodge, yet able when I wanted to to speak the speech of the streets and wear the uniform of the streets. I was a fraud as a street boy, as I was from the beginning fraudulent as the prospective priest of God.

Yet I had nothing else. I stood in the dull light with Conny, my shoulders against the brick wall, a cigarette hanging from my lip, because I had no other home, I belonged nowhere else.

I straightened up, looking to my left at the busy street lined with German cafés, neon signs in all the colors: red, green, blue, violet, some of them moving, some of them flashing on and off. That street on a good night is like a brilliant amusement park when all the clip joints are wide open and the barkers are shilling them in from the street, talking it up through their little megaphones.

The sound of music came into the street through the open doors of bars and cafés, juke-box tunes, xylophone music, the boomp, booomp, booomp of a German band playing that crazy *Schnitzelbank* song that pleases the tourists and service men. The rhythm of the music crept into my blood. I shook off the haunting sadness that had seeped over me a moment ago.

"To hell with Beano Malloy," I said. "Let him sit there and count his money and worry himself into an early grave. The question is, what are we going to do between now and Saturday night without the price of a lousy Coke between us?"

I uttered the words because they were the words that Conny wanted to hear.

"We got to get some money," he said. "We got to get our hands on some dough."

I realized that he was thinking. He leaned against the wall, one hand to his forehead, like a boy in a piece of garden sculpture. The fingers of his other hand moved slowly as if he counted on them. That was Conny thinking, counting his thoughts as they passed slowly through his brain.

"Jackrolling!" he said, snapping his fingers, a conclusion reached. "That's the answer. The only answer."

There were toughs in the neighborhood, older than we, who made a precarious living by rifling the pockets of drunken men on the subway or in parks. Usually the drunks had passed out. Sometimes they were helped to unconsciousness.

"Roll a drunk?" I said. I looked up and down the street. There were city police and service police walking in pairs, watching the whores and the wise guys, always ready for trouble. And I knew that there were plainclothes policemen here and there along the busy street. Conny was out of his mind. I spoke simply to make conversation.

"How can you roll a drunk here?" I asked.

"Not a drunk and not here," said Conny. "You know my brother Al? The one in the Navy?"

I nodded. I knew all the Donovan brothers—the one in the Navy, the one in the Army, the one in the seminary on Staten Island, the one in prison up the river.

"Al told me in the Navy what they do when they're broke is to roll a fag," said Conny earnestly. "They never roll a drunk, only a fag. That way you're in the clear. The faggot can't complain, see? And anyway, who's going to listen to a fag if he does complain? The cops would just belt him one and tell him to be on his way."

That word: fag. Faggot. It is one of my father's words. Of all the things he hates and mistrusts, Jews and college graduates and well-dressed people generally, the thing he hates with true passion is a homosexual, a faggot. He will pronounce the long word: ho-moe-sessual, and he puts enormous contempt into the five syllables. In his mind there is nothing lower on the face of the earth. He had warned me against them many times, especially when he had been drinking.

"A faggot, on East 86th Street?" I said to Conny. "The guys who cruise around here are looking for women, you know that."

"We don't find him here," said Conny. "But I know where we do find him. Al told me where they went, the guys from his ship, when they were in New York last year."

"So where is Fagtown?" I said wearily, bored with Conny by now and fed up with his moronic ideas. I took him no more seriously that night than if he had proposed that we hold up the Chemical Bank and Trust Company.

"West Side," he said eagerly. "They cruise there. Central Park West, around the 70s and 80s."

I looked at the thin, badly nourished face studded with the scars of stubborn acne. He was in earnest. He had proposed the expedition in good faith and as innocently as if he had suggested we go to work in the morning as errand boys for Gristede's Grocery Store. The idea of crime was natural to him, as it was unnatural to me.

"Donovan, are you really that stupid?" I said irritably. "Or are you just crazy?"

"You should talk about being crazy," he said contemptuously.

In a neighborhood like East Yorkville there are no secrets. Adulteries are broadcast in advance. Pregnancies are telegraphed over the rooftop washlines. Everyone who knew me knew that for three weeks after my mother died I had been in the loony bin, the psychiatric hospital. Almost no one mentioned it. I was tempted to hit Conny. I let it go.

"You are full of it, Donovan," I said.

We drifted off in different directions. I walked north for two blocks, turned right, then right again, and entered the choking vestibule of the house in which I lived. I hated the smell of that house. I can smell it now in memory, the smell of age and cheap cookery mixed with the smell of mongrel dogs and the multiplied odors of people. The setting seemed appropriate to rheumatic, impoverished age. Sometimes in the old days I had prayed that we would move away, that the building would burn or fall of its own ancient weight, forcing us to leave the site forever.

For a second I stood in the vestibule, not wanting to go upstairs. The pushbells under the mailboxes stared back malevolently.

It was half past ten. The old man (even now, in memory, I call him that) would be asleep if he had had a tough day at work, or in Murphy's, drinking beer, if he felt all right. On weekday nights he never drank anything but beer. Fridays and Saturdays, if he wanted to, he would put away boilermakers—blended whisky with beer for a chaser. He got drunk sometimes, but it was never an illness with him. It was rather a sign of health. To get drunk on a Saturday night seemed to him a positive virtue. He was never mean unless someone crossed him. In Murphy's they knew enough to leave him alone when he drank whisky. He is a powerful man, trained in unarmed combat and dangerous in a fight.

He was asleep when I came into the apartment, asleep and snoring, an empty beer can on the floor beside his bed. I went into my aunt's room though I knew she wasn't home. It is a small room on the back court with a fire escape outside. It looked empty and very neat, a crucifix over the bed, holy pictures on the walls, starched white curtains at the window, back numbers of the *Catholic Digest* piled up on the table. There was a cheap varnished dresser, the top covered with a clean huck towel.

She should have been a nun, I thought, looking at the bleeding heart on the wall and at the neat narrow bed, the cover pulled tight as a drum, not a wrinkle or a dent on it. My aunt was religious in the way my mother had been religious, and that summer she still believed that I intended to become a priest.

On the rusting steel lattice of the fire escape were slum-bred geraniums in pots. I had promised to water them while my aunt was away at the Carroll Club Camp, and I remembered to do this, bringing water from the kitchen in a big saucepan.

I went into the parlor, a small room crowded with furniture, one window on the airshaft, another on the street, neither of them big enough to let in much light or air. On the wall were colored photographs of Cardinal Spellman and Bishop Sheen. The one of Sheen was signed. They had belonged to my mother, the pictures. On another wall was a gilt frame with my father's medals and his paratrooper's wings, pinned to black velvet under glass. Silver Star, Bronze Star, Purple Heart and the various campaign medals. It was my mother who had them framed, but he hadn't raised any objection and often he stopped to look at the medals with a kind of nostalgic approval.

The only new thing in the parlor was the TV set, shiny new and so big it seemed to take up a quarter of the room. The old man liked it for the fights and my aunt always watched Bishop Sheen and some of the family-type shows. I could do without it ordinarily but that night I turned it on, cutting off the sound because I didn't want to wake the old man.

I sat looking at the silent picture. I didn't pay much attention to what was going on on the screen but having the thing turned on was a comfort. It was like having someone else in the room, someone who moved but made no sound and did not answer back. It was almost like having a dog in the room, a presence that cut the empty feeling you get sometimes when you are alone.

The old man snored away, dead to the world, and the silent figures on the TV screen moved back and forth about their business like shadows. In the parlor there was the faint smell of stale beer; that was the old man's powerful breath.

I sat in the old man's TV chair, lonely and disgusted with myself. There was no need to be lonely. Even at this hour there would be kids on most of the corners. Conny Donovan was down there with his preposterous dreams of wealth through assault and robbery. In a neighborhood like that one it is never necessary to be lonely; you can always find someone you know by name.

But I wanted to be lonely that night. I wanted to sit by myself in the dark with the silent TV in front of my face. I wanted to think about myself. I sat there watching the silent screen, wishing that I would explode. There was something inside me that was like a bomb ticking away, a bomb that no one knew about except myself. I had fooled them all about that, even the clever psychiatrists at the Kips Bay Hospital. If they had found the bomb at the center of my being, they would not have let me go after three weeks to walk out into the bright winter sunlight with my aunt beside me. They would have sent me to the asylum at Central Islip on Long Island, and God knows when they would have turned me loose.

The old man stopped snoring. I heard him roll over in the bed and groan. The springs creaked and I knew that he was sitting up in the bed, my mother's bed, where she had slept and where when I was small I had often slept by her side.

I heard him strike a match and curse. Then he came into the parlor rubbing his eyes. He always slept in his undershirt and he was naked from the waist down. He stretched himself, the cigarette in his mouth, then scratched his chest through the T shirt. He was a big man with very powerful hands and arms, a laboring man for all that he earned more in a week than many a prosperous businessman. There was an animal quality about him, attractive but terrifying. The strong black hair that covered his chest came all the way down the front of his body and joined the hairs of his crotch, tough and wiry like black fur. His skin was ruddy from work in the open. His eyes were like intense blue stones.

"Jesus, it's hot," he complained. "I can't sleep for the heat."

He was born in that tenement flat as I was and he grew up on the streets of Yorkville, but you would have sworn that he had been born in Ireland. It was not an accent but an intonation, an Irish-American intonation, defiant, anachronistic, as if he were saying, *I am a donkey and proud of it. I am a flannelmouth and proud of it.*

Bare feet padding, he went into the kitchen for a can of beer. He came back with the can in his hand and drank from it standing up. I saw the muscles of his throat working as he swallowed the beer, half a can at one go. Then he wiped his mouth with the back of his hand and grinned shyly.

"Like pouring it down a rathole," he said. "There's a Coke in the icebox, Vincent. Why don't you have it before you turn in?"

There was a primary awkwardness between us, aside from the things that ran deeper, that he thought I knew nothing about. At sixteen I was almost an educated man, trained by the awesome Jesuits, while he had left school on his fourteenth birthday to go to work with a hod on his shoulder.

I went to the refrigerator and got the Coke. We sat in the dark, the TV picture still turned on. He finished his beer, got another can and sat down in his big chair, the one I had been using. He put the beer can on the floor.

"Turn up the sound," he said. "We might as well watch the show."

I turned the knob and the sound came up. It was an old movie about halfway through. The old man sat there with his beer and watched. It didn't seem to matter to him that he didn't know what was going on because he had missed the first half. It was something to do, just sitting there in the heat drinking beer, scratching himself, watching the people on the screen, the men in tight double-breasted suits, the women in clothes with padded shoulders.

I sat in a smaller chair and watched him, thinking without any bitterness: This would be his idea of heaven, watching TV, drinking beer, going to Murphy's when he felt like it, going, perhaps, to a whorehouse when the urge came upon him. That and laying brick. He would be satisfied with that forever, *in aeternum*, to the end of time.

Watching my father and my father's body in the cheese-green light of the TV tube I felt my mood shift from benevolent contempt to envy. At least he is his own man, some interior voice reminded me. He commands power in his own limited, dangerous world. He can lay brick as fast and as well as the next man. He has a fierce craft pride. He can fight with his fists better than most. He can drink beer, enough beer to float away the whole of cruddy Yorkville. He can screw a woman. I was sure of that. He can ask for, flatly, and be paid a hundred and sixty dollars a week.

I was money-conscious partly, I suppose, because I had thrown away all of my week's allowance but mostly because the possession of money seemed to express ultimate power. He was like a king with money. He would hand me my allowance, peeling the dirty bills from a thick wad carried in his pocket. I had watched him hand money to my mother in the same way and sometimes, through the window of Murphy's, I had seen him shove it across the bar, carelessly, as if it were rubbish. The bills were dirty, the pocket was dirty, often his hands themselves were dirty, but there was something magnificent and lordly in the way he dispensed money. He created the impression that he would never want for money, that he would always earn it with his two hands.

"Can you get me a job as a helper?" I said. As I spoke my throat tightened and my knees began to tremble.

The old man turned. He couldn't hear me over the sound of the TV. "What's that, Vincent?" he asked.

I switched off the sound. "Can you get me a job as a helper?" I said again.

He shook his head. "Got to have a card," he said. "Got to have a card in the union."

"You can get me a permit card," I said.

"Got to be eighteen, Vincent, you know that," he said, taking another swig of beer.

"I'm big for my age," I said stubbornly. "I could pass for eighteen."

"Why would you want it?" he said. "It's hard work. Dirty work. Why would you want it?"

"For the money," I said. "For something to do."

He shook his head. "Don't work with your hands, Vincent," he said. "For me it's all right. I was brought up to it. It's the only thing I know. But you got an education. You are going to be a priest. You shouldn't be working with your mitts."

I looked down at my hands, then looked at his. His hands were hard as hammers, square as two great tools.

"I could do the work," I said. "Anyway, there are priests and brothers who work with their hands. Christ himself worked with his hands."

I didn't have the courage to tell him that I had renounced my mother's vocation. I wanted to tell him. I wanted to shriek in the hot little room: *I don't even believe in God.* But I didn't have the courage.

"Don't I give you money?" he said. "I give you plenty, you know that. If you want a job get a job in an office where you can use your education."

"You've got to be eighteen for the jobs that are any good," I told him.

"You got to be eighteen to work on the scaffold," he said bluntly. "Now, get me a can of Schaefer's, will you, and let's watch the rest of the show."

I went to the kitchen and got his beer. I speared the can, once, twice, then defiantly I took a gulp from the can. I carried the beer into the parlor and handed it to the old man. He took it without saying thanks, all of his mind on the ancient movie.

"The picture stinks," I said. "I'm going to bed."

"Good night, Vincent," he said, not taking his eyes from the screen.

I stood beside him, aware of the powerful head and shoulders back-lighted by the TV. Doesn't he know that I hate him? I asked myself bitterly. Doesn't he know that I wish he would choke on his frigging beer or drop off the God damned scaffold tomorrow and fall twenty stories to the street? How can you live in the same house with someone who wishes you were dead and not know it?

I turned and went into my bedroom. It was a cubbyhole the size of a cell with a foot-wide window on the airshaft, almost as small as the room in which I sleep now, here in the madhouse in the mountains. There was a narrow bed, a straight chair and a sturdy wooden table that I used for homework during the school year. Last year's books lay in a pile: *Latin, Fourth Year; French Grammar; Trigonometry; Selections for Modern Catholic Readers; The History of Our Country; The Heart of St. Thomas Aquinas.*

On a shelf near the bed were my own books, paperback copies of Joyce and Farrell and Faulkner and Wolfe, Salinger and

Erskine Caldwell. There was a novel by J.-P. Sartre in English and another by Albert Camus. In the Kips Bay Hospital I had started to read all kinds of books that would not have been approved by my mother or the priests at school.

The light bulb dangled from the ceiling, just the wire and a forty-watt bulb. Standing under the light I stripped down. There was a thin film of sweat on my skin so that in the yellow light my body glistened as if it had been rubbed with oil, like that of a Japanese wrestler. I looked at myself in the mirror. In a few weeks I would be seventeen, old enough to quit school if I liked, almost a grown man. I was lean and hard, with a flat stomach and a good pair of shoulders. I could box a little and I knew something about street fighting. It was a thing we learned in Yorkville, the way kids in other sections learn to bow and dance. I was tough enough for my age but I didn't look the way he looked.

He was like a bull, a tough and mean and arrogant bull. He worked like a bull and he drank like a bull, he went into a woman like a bull. I will never look the way he looks, I thought, regarding the reflection of myself in the death-house light of my air-shaft room. There was an old-country look about him, the look of the strong one who had survived where the weak had perished. He was a bull, a powerful Irish bull.

Yet my mother had chosen him. She had taken the bull into her bed of her own free will. On the wall behind my work table was a picture of my mother, a photograph colored by hand. The color was all wrong, fake as a cheap fake rose. Still, it looked like her. The mouth, the eyes, they were like mine, but she had been small and small-boned, not much more than a hundred pounds, and delicate, with narrow hips and slim legs.

When I was a child, sometimes I would be frightened by the dark or by my dreams. She would take me into her bed, hold me until I fell asleep, then carry me back to my own room. I remember the way she felt when she held me, the small waist and small hands, the small breasts upon which I rested until I fell asleep.

I stood in my room and stared at her picture, thinking of her body beneath the body of the big bull in the next room with his beer breath and his black fur and his big square hands, thinking: He was too big for her. He must have torn her to pieces. Almost broken her in two. My imagination was vivid and close to the obscene. There was no mercy in me on that hot night.

I looked at the picture. There is a song: "The Rose of Tralee." Whenever I heard it I thought of my mother. She is lovely and fair as the rose of the summer. But 'twas not her beauty alone that won me.

The pale crystal fountain that stands in the beautiful Vale of Tralee.

Why would she marry a bull like that? my soul demanded of my mind. The bull with his strong black fur that went right down from his thick neck to the private parts of his body. I loved my mother who was dead and I loved no one else. I could love no one else. My father who lived I feared and hated. He was my antagonist who could never be defeated.

In the other room near his framed medals was a photograph of him made when he was a young soldier, in 1942 or 1943. He was thinner then and better looking, but the strain of the bull was on the young face too.

When he was drunk in a certain way he would talk about the war, mostly about a place called Arnhem, where he had been dropped from the sky with the 82nd Airborne Division. On that day, in an afternoon he killed sixteen Germans, and two of them he killed with his bare, square hands.

"I broke their necks," he would say when he was drunk. "I broke their dirty Kraut necks with these two hands."

Then he would hold out his hands so that people could see how strong they were and then, after a little while, he would go into his crying jag.

"I'm sorry I did it," he would say. "What the hell. They were men like other men, if they were Germans. One of them was a Catholic, I know that. I saw the medal around his neck. I'm sorry I killed them. I am."

He was sorry he killed them but killing them and the others had got him his Silver Star, and that he kept hanging on the wall pinned to a piece of black velvet that my mother had sewn with her own hands.

I stood in my airless room and cursed him. He was a murderer. He had murdered those Germans with his hands, and he had murdered my mother, killed her (I believed it!) just as surely as if he had strangled her, broken her neck in the paratrooper's way as he had broken the German necks.

I had heard them. I had seen it all. I had been the unknown witness and I had seen it all in the sick light that came through my mother's bedroom window.

Even now through my calm it is a scene that causes pain. I want to evade it, to cut it from the film. It will not be cut. It is central to the spoilt rhetoric of my childhood. My stomach tightens here in the madhouse dark, the safe dark. My viscera turn inside my body and feel as if they now contain shards of broken glass.

It will not be evaded. My mind comes into focus. It sets the scene.

When my mother was alive she slept alone, in the bed he uses now. He slept on a couch in the front room. I slept in my room on the airshaft.

I was in bed but I was awake even though it was almost three o'clock in the morning. I heard him come in from Murphy's saloon with his load on. He looked into my room at me and

I pretended to be asleep. I could hear him in the front room getting out of his clothes. Then I heard him padding around. He opened the door to my mother's room. I sat up in my bed and listened. Then I crawled out of the bed and knelt on the floor beside my door. I could see him over my mother's bed, stark naked in the light from the window. And I could hear them both.

"Mike, you know I can't risk it," my mother said. "Dr. Gorman said it might kill me if I was to have another child."

"I'll use something," he said. "I've got them here."

"It's against God's law," she said, her voice full of fear.

"For the love of God, woman, I'm human," he said. "For the love of Christ, I'm only human."

His big bull's body was over her.

"Mike, please, for the sake of Vincent," she said, pleading with him.

"Ah, the hell with Vincent," he said. "Am I a man or not? Am I a human being or not? Do you want to drive me to a whorehouse? Is that what you want?"

"I can't refuse you," she said. "Whatever Dr. Gorman says, I can't refuse you. I am your wife, and I know what my duty is. But you mustn't use those things."

I saw it all. I saw his big body pumping in the sick yellow light from the street lamp that came through the bedroom window. I heard the bed creaking and groaning, and I heard the bull: "Ah, Jesus, I love you. Sweet Jesus, I love you."

He loved her, the bull, so he killed her, I thought, standing in my fetid little room.

She had a rheumatic heart, a thing that can take you like that, and it took her, three months pregnant, on an October afternoon as she stood in the cockroach kitchen.

I came home from school at half past three and found her on the kitchen floor. There was a pot on the stove boiling away, filling the kitchen with fragrant steam. On the floor beside her was a spoon, a big spoon that she used to stir things with when she was cooking. I stood at the kitchen door with my schoolbag in my hand. I tried to scream but there wasn't any sound. Then I dropped the bag and ran to where she was lying on the floor. I held her in my lap rocking her back and forth as if I could rock her back to life.

She was dead.

She was almost cold.

I wouldn't believe it. I couldn't believe it. I didn't run for the doctor or even for Mrs. Mulleady who lived on the first floor. I just sat there near the kitchen stove and held her in my arms for nearly three hours until my father came home. He had stopped at Murphy's on the way. You could smell the beer on his breath.

"Don't touch her," I said. "You son of a bitch, don't you touch her."

He moved toward us, then stopped.

"Mother of God!"

He crossed himself, then knelt beside us, trying to touch her cheek. I went off my head. My teeth sank into the back of his hand. If I could have killed him I would have done it. He fought with me and I fought back, using my teeth and my fingernails. Finally he kicked me hard in the stomach and I went flying across the room. My mother lay on the kitchen floor. I was sick from the kick in the stomach. I smelt the bug juice on the kitchen linoleum. Then I passed out.

When I came to I was on my bed. My aunt was there and so was Dr. Gorman. I could hear but I couldn't speak. I couldn't move or make a sound.

"Catatonia," Gorman said.

"I shouldn't have kicked him," the old man said. "I don't know. I lost my head."

"It wasn't the kick," Dr. Gorman said. "It was the shock. We see this. I saw it myself during the war. You must have seen it, Mike. He'll come out of it all right, but he'll have to have treatment. In a hospital."

"Not Bellevue!"

That was my aunt. She had a black fear of Bellevue, born somewhere in her Irish past. In her mind it was a place where people went to die.

"The private places cost a fortune," Dr. Gorman said.

"Never mind the money," my aunt said.

"Never mind what it costs," said the old man.

So they sent me to the Kips Bay Hospital, a brand-new shiny booby hatch incorporated strictly for profit, potted palms and fake lilies in the glossy stone-and-chrome lobby and upstairs wire mesh at the windows and guards all over the place. They called them aides but they were guards, "attendants," as we have them here. Whatever you wanted—a match to light your cigarette, a trip to the john, a drink of water, a comb and brush, your belt in the morning—you had to ask an attendant for it.

The bill was forty dollars a day. The treatment was pretty dramatic. They put electrodes on your head and shoot a charge through your brain. First it stirs things up, and then they settle down again. The idea is that they will settle down into a more satisfactory arrangement.

I don't know. I know that when I came out of the hospital with my aunt beside me into the bright November day I was different. It wasn't the shock treatment that did it. I did it myself in my own mind. I had had plenty of time to think and to talk to the other patients, the drug addicts, alcoholics, homosexuals, all mixed up together, separated in that hospital not by age or the character of the illness but, for convenience, by tractability, the tough nuts on the top floor, the almost well on the lowest floor, the others ranged on the floors between.

I was different. For one thing I had lost my faith in God, violently and all at once. It had been God and the Church that had forced my mother into the things that made her die. What kind of God would do that? my intelligence asked my soul. Only a monster. There was no God.

For another thing there was my father, the old man. I had always been afraid of him. He had always seemed a sweaty giant stepping between myself and my mother. In the Kips Bay Hospital I had decided that he was a bull and that I hated him.

The bull.

Once at the Catholic Youth Camp we had sneaked off over the hills to a farm where the bull had been brought to service half a dozen cows. We had watched this fascinated. It was a violent, educative scene, the bull and the cow in the hot New Jersey sun. It stuck in the mind.

He is a bull, I had decided sitting in the slick day room of the psychiatric hospital. There was nothing to the bull but a brute body and the brute sex, so enormous, so realistic that it scared you. That is my old man, I thought, a powerful body, powerful balls and nothing else, nothing on this earth else except the ability to lay brick and to drink beer until it was running out of his ears. He had killed my mother with his big bull's body and that meant that I was alone in the world, without a friend in the world that I cared about.

I thought of all these things that summer night after I had left Donovan, lying on my narrow bed in the narrow airshaft room. With the light off, that room was black as a coal mine. No light came in through the airshaft. After a while, when my eyes got used to the dark, I saw a slit of gray light at the bottom of the closed door. It came from the TV. Through the door I could hear the sound, just a blur of voices. I couldn't catch the words except during the commercials, when the station volume was stepped up.

My mind drifted in the dark, remembering Conny Donovan standing against the brick wall, filled with tough kid talk.

"What we oughta do is roll a fag."

Conny was as simple-minded as his brother the thief who was rotting in a cell in Sing Sing Prison. I knew that. The idea was absurd. Still, I could not get the raw phrase out of my mind.

"What we oughta do is roll a faggot."

A faggot.

I uttered the word under my breath. Then I realized that I wasn't quite sure what it was that a faggot did. I knew in a crude, general way, of course, but I didn't really know any more than I really knew what it was that men and women did with each other. I had seen it with my own eyes. I could have drawn you a picture. But I didn't really know. I had never done more with a girl than feel her up outside her clothes, mostly in the movies. Once, in a movie house alone, I sat next to a woman. She was thirty-five, maybe forty. Her hand moved stealthily, but her eyes remained fixed on the wide screen. She took my hand, drawing it toward her, placing it on her knee. I felt the brittle texture of her cheap nylon stocking. Then I became sick with fear and pulled my hand away as if my fingers had been burnt. She took her hand away. When she got up I followed her out of the theater, though I had seen only half of the picture. I walked behind her for a few blocks fascinated by the movement of her body. She stopped in the street and turned. "Go away, sonny, you're wasting your time," she said. "I have to go home and feed the kids and get ready for my old man."

"What about me?" I said, feeling that somehow she was responsible for me.

"Who cares?" she said. "Go home and try do-it-yourself, you little punk."

I did that. I guess everybody did that. And since my mother had died I had tried to make out with the girls in the show. The newspapers were filled with stories about high school kids and their sex lives. Maybe some kids, colored kids or Puerto Rican kids, but not the kids I ran around with in Yorkville. The neighborhood girls were Catholic kids and the ones I knew were virgins. Of all the boys I knew that summer—twenty, maybe twenty-five fellows—only two had scored for sure, and that was when a bunch of older guys had lined up on a feeble-minded kid down by the river. They let the two young guys in on it just for laughs.

But Conny Donovan, Beano, the rest of the fellows I knew, they were the same as myself no matter how many lies they told. We talked a lot but we really didn't know anything for sure, because a thing like that: it is like getting killed or killing someone. You don't really know anything about it until you have done it yourself or had it done to you.

"What we oughta do is roll a fag."

Donovan's words supplied themselves in the dark, hot air of my little room. I sat up in the bed and called out viciously: "Jesus! Jesus Christ!"

The door to my bedroom opened. In the doorway the old man stood, his body outlined in the cold green moonlight of the TV.

"What's the matter?" he said. "I heard you yell. If you can't sleep, come and watch the show."

"I had a nightmare," I told him. "I just woke up for a minute."

"You ought to get your sleep," he said.

He closed the door. I heard the floorboards creak as he padded into the kitchen for beer, then padded back to his chair in the parlor, set square before the TV.

I lay on my bed that was by now soaked with my sweat. The sight of my old man's powerful sex had started a fatal train of thought. Images rose in my darkened mind. There was my mother, pale as a flower. There was the brass-haired woman from the movie house. There was the hawk-voiced Jesuit priest with his "For-r-r-nication!" A snatch of thigh illegally seen. The cheap ribbed underclothes of an adolescent girl. The smell of cheap adolescent cosmetics. My mind is a sewer, I said to myself. A dirty sewer.

I saw myself standing at the altar dressed in lace, and then in the half-dream I saw myself in the drafty church in full erection. To serve mass. I was not fit to serve mass.

I had lost my faith in God, but the awareness of sin remained. It had been planted too firmly to be uprooted suddenly, as faith had been uprooted. "For-r-r-nication!" What had happened in the movie house with the middle-aged woman was a sin. What I thought at that moment was a sin. Masturbation was a sin.

I was bathed in sin, soaked in it, and the sense of it scalded my flesh, yet I embraced it there in the narrow bed. It was thrilling. It was gorgeous. It was blessed in relief as death. Yet I was aware of terror too as I drove myself homeward, my body enchanted by the fact of sex. I was filled with fear that I would make some sound in the darkness that would attract my father's attention, make him come to the door again.

I made no sound that my father could hear. He did not come to the door again. Exhausted, I closed my eyes on the sweaty pillow and the tears of my eyes mixed with the sweat, but finally I slept.

CHAPTER THREE

I SAY to Dorion: "Sometimes I feel guilty because I am happy without God, without the thought of God."

We stand together in a field of beans, farming tools in our hands. We are trusted inmates, working outside the walls, but a guard in a dark-blue uniform stands on a ridge at the verge of the field. The beans are plump with life. The cultivated earth is fragrant. Dorion smiles and says nothing. He believes in God. Not the God of his fathers or of mine, but in God the Father. It is one of the things we talk about when we are not playing chess.

To believe in God. To serve God. To serve Mass. To refuse to serve.

It was my first truly decisive act after the death of my mother. The morning after I lost all my money to Beano Malloy I called on Father Murtagh.

Father Murtagh's study was air-conditioned. The box in the window hummed dispassionately, offering a steady ration of chilled stale air. The sunlight and the heat of the day were cut off by heavy maroon curtains drawn across the tall, old-fashioned windows. I sat in an easy chair beside the priest's big desk. The dank air from the window box fell upon my naked arms. I shuddered and rubbed my skin.

Father Murtagh wore a cassock. There was the black cassock, the big hands, the ruddy, memorial head. He was a young-ish athletic priest who had been a cross-country runner at Holy Cross. Over the bar in Murphy's saloon there is a picture of him in running clothes breaking through the woods outside of Worcester.

"Surely it's an honor to serve Mass," he said. "And for a boy whose mother hoped he would be a priest—"

He broke off. His long, thin fingers drummed on the polished top of his desk. He smelled of the church next door, a grim, gray granite building more like a jail than a church. The smell of the church was on his cassock, even on his hair and skin—a faint, sickly odor of wax and oil and incense.

"I can't serve Mass any longer," I said.

"But why, Vincent?" Father Murtagh asked, his forehead wrinkled. He picked up a briar pipe from his desk, admired it and put it down. "Why?"

"My thoughts are impure," I said after a few seconds. I wanted to say out loud, "I don't believe in God." But I couldn't do it. I was afraid. It was the cassock and the smell of the church, and it was fear of the neighborhood. There were no atheists in Irish Yorkville. I couldn't say what I wanted to say. I could only stubbornly make my point: I would no longer serve Mass for Father Murtagh or anyone else.

"I will hear your confession," the priest said. "Now, if you like. This evening. Tomorrow."

"No," I said. "I am not prepared."

I left the cool wedge of air in the study and went into the street. The air of the city struck me suddenly after twenty minutes in the chilled room. For a minute or so I stood by the church, feeling the heat that came from the stone.

It was Wednesday, but I was struck by a sudden urge to go and see my mother's grave, though ordinarily my aunt and I went there on Saturdays. I had no money. In the hot sun of noontime I walked back to the apartment and searched in the corners of the kitchen for bottles, a kid's trick. There were nearly a dozen bottles, Coke bottles, deposit beers, four ginger ale bottles that my aunt had left in a neat row beside the refrigerator. I carried them all to the grocery store and got a handful of silver for them, enough to carry me back and forth with a few cents left over for flowers bought from the Greek in the subway.

The Catholic cemeteries in Manhattan have been filled for a long time. My mother was buried in the Bronx, at some distance from Yorkville. The ride was tedious and the subway car was like a long bake oven, paddle fans churning the soupy air. There was a climb uphill to the cemetery gates which were made of iron painted black and gilt, attached to square stone bastions. At night these gates were drawn and locked. I had never questioned the practice before, but on that day as I mounted the hill it struck me as grotesque that the buried dead were locked away.

My mother's grave was raw and new. The grass seed had not caught well and the sinking mound of earth was patchy as if the soil itself were leprous. I placed my cheap bouquet on the earth near the headstone, then stepped back to a respectful distance and knelt upon the warm soil. Mary Elizabeth Catherine McCaffery. For St. Catherine of Siena. I read the words carved into the granite. Beloved wife of Michael James McCaffery. R.I.P.

Without thinking I crossed myself, then realized that mechanically I had been mouthing the words of a prayer. I broke it off angrily. Then I touched the mound of earth with the palms of my hands. The silent earth was feverish under the high sun. "She is not here," I said to myself. "She is not here."

I wept but she did not come. The earth was quiet and beneath the earth rested my mother's remains. She did not come to me in my pain or call to me that I might come to her, as she had done in the past, when I was small. The sense of desertion was profound. Somehow I had hoped that I would find her there, but there was nothing ... a stone cut into the shape of a cross, a mound of earth badly planted, the wilting flowers I had brought with me, already curling in the heat. Wherever she is she is not here, I thought. Yet I spoke to her and I spoke aloud.

"I asked him to get me a job," I said. "He laughed at me. He told me to use my education. What good is my education now?"

I cried bitter tears and they fell to the earth. She was not there. "I am not going to serve Mass for Father Murtagh any more," I said.

I couldn't say what I wanted to say any more than I could say it to Father Murtagh or to my own father. I could not utter the words and let them fall on my mother's grave. My own conviction was absolute. I knew with blinding certainty that I would never again believe in God. But I could not form the words and speak them. Even in the secrecy of my own mind I could not put the words into sequence.

What cannot be expressed in words, tossed out on the empty air or into the mind of another, perhaps must be expressed in action. I know that as I knelt beside the grave I was frightened of my own potential. I had no God but I had the sense of sin, and where the sense of sin exists the idea of evil exists. It must be fought or embraced.

She was not there. Beneath the mound were her flesh and bones, already decomposing, eager to return to the soil itself. My mother was not there. My sense of her absence was violent, yet I remained beside her grave until it was time for the cemetery gates to be locked and an old man in brass buttons touched me gently on the shoulder.

I rode back to Manhattan on the subway, aware of the need to do something, to take some action. I thought of suicide. I could jump from the roof of the house we lived in and land on the cracked cement. I could get a gun somehow and destroy my brain. That would put a stop to things, I thought, swaying as the subway car moved around a long, screeching curve.

I had a sense of nausea and a mindless need to make something happen. I could not face the sequence of humid weeks, of faceless days. I had changed inside and I wanted somehow to reveal this change to myself in terms of action.

"What we oughta do is roll a faggot!"

Donovan's words came into my mind with shocking force, expunging the visions of my suicide. To roll a fag. To commit a crime. In the sick heat of the subway car the prospect of violence was attractive, dark random violence, related to murder.

"What, we oughta do is roll a faggot!"

The hot brakes howled in the subway tunnel and the long train came to a shuddering stop. It was 86th Street. I left the train and climbed the staircase to the street, passing the Greek florist's stand where I had bought my mother's bouquet. The flowers were wilting in the airless heat and their heavy perfume was nauseating.

I walked east toward my own neighborhood. I hadn't eaten since breakfast but I didn't feel hungry. It was an hour before darkness and already the neon signs were on, brilliant as cheap synthetic jewels, junk jewelry designed to be worn by a gigantic whore. I passed the German cabarets, ornamented with thousands of steins and painted heraldic shields. A snatch of violent rock and roll, torn off, came through the door of a bar as I passed.

Conny Donovan stood alone on the corner of 86th and York. He stood in the warm twilight, holding up the wall of the building, broke, with nothing to do. I stopped and stood beside him.

"Where you been the whole day?" he asked petulantly.

I didn't want to tell him I had been to the cemetery; that was a thing to be done in good clothes, formally, on a Saturday or Sunday.

"Busy," I said mysteriously.

"You get any money?" he said.

I shook my head, studying Donovan's ravaged cheeks, pitted and scarred like the face of the moon seen through the high-powered telescope.

"Were you serious last night about rolling a fag?" I said.

The words seemed to supply themselves, but they were monstrously logical once they had been spoken. They expressed my desperate need for change, for violent and conclusive change.

Donovan was startled. Last night he had been talking just to hear himself talk. Now he was trapped. If he backed out now, he knew that I would have him pegged for a phony, and Donovan was jealous of his prestige as any war lord in China.

"Sure I was serious," he said. "Whadda you think?"

"You've got a partner," I said. "When do we start?"

He looked at me suspiciously. "You trying to kid me or something?" he said.

"I mean it," I told him. "It's your scheme, so you be the general."

Donovan was stupid but his mind had its own slow-witted logic. He improvised, drawing on his ratlike intelligence, remembering things he had heard from his brothers.

"First we catch ourselves a ride across the park at 86th," he said. "Then we'll make up the scheme when we see how things look."

We hopped a bus going west, hanging on to the rear end, dropping off at the red lights, hopping back on again just as the bus started to roll. In the hot night the stink of the rear-end engine made me sick. My fingers ached. I hadn't hopped buses for a long time, figuring that it was a thing for little kids. I had forgotten how rugged it was.

At Fifth Avenue the bus pulled up and we dropped off.

"This is murder," I said. "I hope we ride back inside the bus."

Conny shook his head. "We ride back in a cab, jerk, all the way to the East Side."

He was like a slum-bred dog scenting petty violence. We both laughed and climbed back on the rear end of the bus. We were excited then and not very scared. I don't think either of us knew exactly what we were doing. It was just a crazy idea that Donovan had heard from his brother the sailor. It was something to do instead of standing on the corner leaning against the wall.

"So here's what we do," Conny said when we were standing in the dark on the western border of Central Park. "We do it just the way Al said the Navy guys do it. You're the best-looking one between us on account of my pimples, so you be bait." He bent down and picked up a good-sized rock from the ground. "You sit on that bench there and wait for a fag to pick you up. Con him along, like. Suck him in. I'll be behind you with this."

He hefted the rock, then tossed it from one hand to the other.

"You're the general," I said. "But it sounds crazy to me."

"You just sit on the bench and wait," said Conny. "My brother Al is no dope."

I sat in the darkness under a tree, the pale light from the street lamp just touching my face. It was one of the old-style lamps and the light had a greenish cast so that the street looked like a morgue. It is a wide, modern street, park on one side, big slab-faced apartment houses on the other. On the other side of the street people were walking up and down, getting in and out of cabs, coming and going from the big houses. Doormen stood under the canvas canopies.

The park side where I sat was deserted and very dark. Three Puerto Rican kids passed and gave me the onceover. Conny is crazy, I thought. Or else his brother Al is crazy. Still, I thought,

Al was in the Navy and people are always talking about sailors and queers.

I sat in the hot summer night breathing in the smell of the park mixed with the smell of exhaust from the street, waiting, not quite knowing what I waited for, half thinking that the whole idea was crazy.

It wasn't so crazy.

After a while a man stopped and sat down on the bench beside me. He was about thirty, a well-dressed man wearing a dark silk suit and a light-colored silk tie. He crossed his legs and I could see the shine on his shoes glistening in the light from the street lamp. His crossed leg moved nervously. Then he lit a cigarette with a Zippo lighter that made a big flame and I could see his face. He had a crew cut and neat, regular features. He looked like any young businessman you might see coming out of an office building on Madison Avenue, an out-of-towner turned New Yorker, clean-cut and prosperous. If he is a homo, I thought, you can't tell it by looking at him. He took a few puffs on his cigarette, making the tip gleam in the dark, then said pleasantly, "Would you like a cigarette, son?"

"Sure," I said.

He offered me the pack with one pulled out so that I could take it easily. I put the cigarette into my mouth and he held the lighter for me, keeping the orange flame burning for a few seconds after my cigarette was lit. He was looking me over. Sizing me up. Then he snapped the Zippo shut. It is silver, I thought, pure silver, not chromium plate like the standard Zippos.

"It is a hot night," he said. "It reminds me of the tropics. Of Nassau in the Bahamas. Have you ever been there?"

I shook my head. Conny had told me to wait for the guy to make the moves. The idea was, if I was too eager he might get suspicious. We sat in the dark for a few minutes, smoking.

Behind us the park was dark and silent. The long, wide street was silent too, traffic moving steadily, making no sound except for the swish of tires on asphalt and sometimes the screech of brakes when somebody pulled up sharp for a red light. Underneath the silence I could hear the sound of the city. It was purring like a giant cat, throbbing in the hot night, millions and millions of people all together on a narrow island just living and breathing, creating a sound as if the city had a life of its own beyond the lives of the millions of people with a heart of its own and a great body that purred like a cat. There was an actual sound I could hear like the sound of the dynamos you see from the street when you pass the Edison Company power station on the East River.

"It's hot like this in Nassau," the man said. "Hot and moist. But down there the atmosphere is heavy with the smell of the flowers so that you would think someone had sprayed the air with perfume. It is a sultry and beautiful island in the warm weather. It smells like a woman, a passionate woman, naked and moist and heavy with perfume, ready to spread her legs for the first man who comes along."

I could feel it ... the build-up. My mouth was dry. The man looked at me in the dim light, then said, "Have you ever been with a woman? In the bed, I mean?"

"Sure, lot's of times," I said. "What do you think I am?"

It was a lie, but I would have told the same lie to almost anyone who asked me except perhaps my Aunt Theresa. If my father had asked the question I would have given the same answer.

The man moved toward me on the bench, then put a hand on my thigh. My heart was pounding. I felt the raw sexual excitement as if I had been sitting with a girl in the back rows of the movie house. Maybe I am queer, I thought, and too dumb to know it. I moved a little on the bench. The man squeezed my thigh, using just a little pressure. It could mean something, it could mean nothing.

"What was she like?" he said. "Was she young? A girl? Or a real woman?"

"She was all right," I said.

"Did you put it in her?" he said. "Right in her?"

He was close to me now and his hands moved up my thigh until his fingers touched me. Play it cool, Conny had said. I wanted to push the fingers away but I couldn't. It was as if I was paralyzed. The man went on talking, his fingers moving gently all the time. There was a clean smell about him of shaving lotion and soap. I remember thinking: I should smash him one. That had been my father's advice. "Kick him in the place where it will hurt him the most," the old man had said. "Then run like hell for a cop."

I didn't move. I sat with the heated city around me, touched in the flesh by positive evil, fascinated and repelled.

"Would you like to go into the park?" said the man. "It's cooler there, and I know a nice place where we can sit and where no one can see us."

"It's all right here," I said. I felt a little thrill of fear.

"It's nicer in the park," the man said, his fingers moving again. "Much nicer."

"Okay," I said.

We both stood up. I was five feet ten, that summer. He was taller than I was, with a nice pair of shoulders, and he must have outweighed me by forty pounds. I hope Donovan knows what he's doing, I thought. I can never handle this guy on my own. If he knows any tricks he may give the two of us trouble. Then I thought: we can always run. Worse comes to worst, we can always run.

The man took my arm, holding my elbow in his hand, the way you would hold the arm of a girl. I didn't like it but I didn't pull away from him.

"Come on, I'll show you the place," he said. "You'll like it."

We entered the park by a stone gate and followed a path that led downhill. Under the trees the park was dark. Way off, for an instant, you could see the lights of the East Side. Then we dipped into the park and there was nothing but the dark trees and bushes and the smell of dirt that had been spaded up and covered with horse manure. I couldn't hear Conny behind us and I was scared. Then I remembered that Conny was wearing sneakers, as I was, and that I shouldn't have heard him anyway. The man beside me wore shoes with hard leather heels and they made a clop-clop sound on the pavement, almost like the sound of a woman's high heels on the sidewalk.

We turned into a narrower path, so narrow that the bushes on either side grazed my cheeks as I walked. Off to the right was a patch of water. The moonlight struck the water surface so that it flashed like glass. We came to a small cleared space in the bushes. There was a bench and behind that a little stone fountain and above that the statue of somebody, made of white stone that showed up in the black night.

"This is the place," the man said. "Do you like it?"

"What is there to like?" I said. "It's a bench in the bushes. So what?"

"It's private," he said. "No one can see us here. You can do anything you want here and when we walk out of the park no one will know what you did."

I had a ready-made answer for that one. I will know, I might have told him. God will know. I said nothing. I agreed with the man. If no one could see us then whatever we did would be left behind us when we walked out of the park. If you kill someone in a secret place, my mind whispered in the darkness, and you don't tell anyone about it, then it is just exactly as if it didn't happen, if that is the way you want it to be. It's just as if you stepped on a roach, then kicked him under the kitchen stove. Once he is under that stove it is just as if there had never been a roach.

Doing wrong meant getting caught. The idea struck me with the force of a hammer, seeming to be in the hot night profound, harshly simple and original with me.

The man moved toward me in the darkness. His face and hands were white as chalk against the black soft night, white as the statue over his head carved out of stainless alabaster. It was hot and I could smell the grass and the bushes and the warm earth, the soil of the park still fermenting as it relinquished the heat of the day. The man touched me. The rude pass. Then he put both hands on my cheeks.

"You're a handsome boy," he said. "Innocent and brave and proud." He moved closer. I backed away. He laughed.

I sat on the bench. I was scared and faintly nauseous. The man sat beside me, touching me with his fingers again. He was breathing hard now the way the girls breathed in the movies. He is hot as a pistol, I thought, suddenly almost dispassionate. He is hot as a red-hot stove.

"You are an angel," he said. "A little angel. I could kiss you all over."

He slipped from the bench to the ground. I saw his face for a split second. In that funny light it was like the face of an animal, a rat gnawing its way from a box. The sound he made was like the sound of an animal in a trap. I was terrified but I was fascinated.

Then Conny came out of the bushes fast, like a halfback cutting into the clear, sure-footed on his rubber-soled shoes. His arm came up, the stone in his hand, then it came down fast. The stroke of a hammer, precise, conclusive. I heard the sound as the rock struck the back of the man's skull, like the sound that is made when you kick a heavy wooden box. The man went down. I was on my feet and then I stood there trembling.

"Jesus, you killed him," I said. "Christ, Donovan, you killed the guy."

"Killed him my ass," Conny said. He showed me the rock that was still in his hand. He had wrapped a handkerchief around it, making a pad.

The man lay on his stomach. Conny rolled him over. "Get his watch and his ring," he said. "I'll get his wallet."

I did what Conny said, taking the ring and the watch and the silver lighter. Then I stood up, swaying, touching the stone wall for support. I looked down at the man. He was alive, all right. I could see that now. Conny had just knocked him cold. His mouth hung open and he drooled. He looked disgusting. There was a force that rose in me, murderous and precise. I felt the soul inside me tighten. I drew back my foot and kicked the man in the stomach. I wanted to kill him, to kick him to death.

"You dirty queer," I yelled. "You dirty rotten stinking faggot."

Conny's hand was over my mouth. He was all business. "Shut up, you jerk," he whispered. "Do you want to bring on the cops?"

I shook myself free and kicked the man again, saying nothing, just kicking the man in the soft part of his behind. Then my thighs seemed to flood and I stood there, helpless. Conny grabbed me and we ran until we reached the main path. We pulled up short under a sallow park lamp. I had the watch and the ring in my hand. Donovan seized them.

"Let's get out of the God-damned park before the guy comes to," he said.

We went out of the park and turned north. The wide street looked just the same, people coming and going on the other side, the park side empty and dark.

"Let's get a cab," I said. Now that the thing was over with I wanted to quit the area as quickly as possible.

"We better take a bus," Conny decided. "A cab is no good right now. Hackies write down their calls."

He took a dollar from the wallet and we caught the bus at 86th Street. At Madison Avenue we got off. We stood on the strange street corner filled with pride, all the fear gone out of us. Conny was pleased with himself. The general. I felt something different: a chilling, inhuman, metallic satisfaction with myself that was precise as the stab of a hypodermic needle. I had almost killed someone. I had wanted to kill him, and what resulted in my own heart was a burning sense of life. Here in the madhouse I pause for a moment and reconstruct what I felt. It was a dangerous sensation, related to what must be felt by prizefighters and racing drivers and soldiers who love war for itself. It was the thrill of the bull ring. The act itself had been criminal, unlicensed, but somehow nevertheless as formalized as bull-killing, permissible as the sniper's bullet or the parachutist's fatal embrace of his opponent's neck.

There was a food shop a few yards away, an imitation Hamburger Heaven, with thick gold letters on the plate-glass windows and pine paneling inside. We ordered two hamburgers, then went to the men's room. We went into the place where you sit down and locked the door behind us. Conny took out the wallet and counted the money quickly. Then he whistled. "Forty-four bucks," he said. "Holy Jesus, McCaffery, we're rich."

He handed me twenty-two dollars. I tucked the money into the little pocket of my blue jeans. We went out of the john and sat at the counter, eating the eighty-cent hamburgers. As soon as I tasted the meat and the ketchup and the good soft roll, I felt all right again. It was just the way I had said it in my mind—as if you had stepped on a cockroach and kicked him under the stove.

"What about the watch and the ring?" I said when we came out of the hamburger place and started east toward our own neighborhood.

"We better play it smart and get rid of them," Conny said. "If we try to hock them we might get into a jam."

"I need a watch," I said. "Why don't I keep it?"

Conny was too smart for that. "What will you tell the guys on the block?" he said. "What will you tell your old man? That you found it? A hundred-dollar watch? Don't be a jerk, McCaffery. Money they can't trace. So we won it in a crap game. They may not believe it, but how can they prove it? Anybody can have money. It's all the same. But watches, jewelry, that kind of stuff, it's a lead-pipe cinch to trace."

"You told me to take it," I insisted.

"I was wrong," said Conny. "Next time we only take money, okay?"

The watch and the ring and the wallet and the solid silver lighter we threw into the East River. The wallet was full of credit cards. The lighter was engraved with an initial. We put them into a tin can weighted down with rocks and walked out onto the 59th Street bridge and dropped them into the greasy water.

I hated to let go of the watch and the lighter, but I saw that Conny was right. He was stupid but methodical, and after all one of his brothers was a professional thief.

Standing on the bridge we counted the money again just for the sake of feeling it in our fingers. It was more money than either of us had ever held in his hands before.

At Christmas time when I, was twelve, my Aunt Theresa gave me a ten-dollar bill folded into a little envelope with an oval window so you could see the picture of Alexander Hamilton as if it was in a frame. The day after Christmas my old man took it away from me. "Ten bucks is too much for a kid like you to handle," he said. "I'll give it to you a buck a week."

I didn't argue with him. How can you argue with a donkey? I thought. Every week for ten weeks he gave me a dirty, wrinkled dollar bill out of his dirty, wrinkled pocket. I never had to remind him and in the end I got all of my aunt's ten-dollar present, but it wasn't the same thing.

"With this kind of dough in our hands we should be a cinch to make a score," Conny said reflectively.

I made no comment. My eyes were fixed on a lighted tow of barges moving slowly down the East River. They were empty coal barges moving away from the power station, but the sight of the maritime arrangement of lights borne on the breast of the diseased river roused in me the urge to adventure, the yearning for some commitment that would carry me out into the huge naked world.

"Worse comes to worse, with this kind of money we could always go to a cat house," Conny said, riffling the bills in his hands.

"I heard you, Conny," I said.

"What's the matter, man, don't you want to get laid?" Conny said eagerly, grabbing my forearm. "Don't you want to make a home run?"

"Sure I do," I said roughly, brushing away Donovan's hand. "What do you think I am?"

CHAPTER FOUR

"WHAT do you think I am?" I had said.

I stand in the sun on the rising land where the farm reaches toward the soft, moist hills. I am the celibate inmate, continent as the Trappist monk on the can of honey my mother bought. I am chaste here, yet I lack for nothing, but that summer I burned with sex. I was invaded, besieged by sex. It tormented me by night, plagued me by day. The sight of a section of naked thigh, seen for an instant on the subway, sent me into a hog wallow. It was an ache, a physical ache, groin-centered, but also sickness of the soul.

We had the money in our blue jeans, but the money did not contain the magic Donovan had anticipated. Every night for a week we went to the movies, sitting in the back rows of various darkened and suggestive theaters trying to pick up girls and sometimes older women. The response was poor. We were engaged in the quarrel with Eve but we were the wrong age. We were too young to be of interest to girls with whom there was something doing and too old to be satisfied with fooling around in the back of the show.

What we sought were wantons, or failing that, honest whores. The wantons were lacking in Yorkville and the only whore we found laughed in our faces. She was a tough little German girl, imported by a soldier and promptly deserted, so that in search of a living she haunted the bars along East 86th Street.

"You think I rob the cradle, hein?" she said, when we showed her our money. "Go on, *kinder.* Vamoose!"

Days we went to Coney Island, cruising along the broadwalk, sometimes going on rides like kids, or spending quarters in the shooting galleries. I had been taught to shoot at school and I liked it. I liked the feel of the smooth stock against my cheek and the gentle kick of the low-powered charge as I squeezed the trigger. It was a means of expression for me but Donovan was bored with it.

"I want to get laid, man," he complained, spitting into the Atlantic Ocean. "I mean really laid."

It's a funny thing, I remember thinking standing beside Donovan, arms on the railing, facing the sea. You read about it in books. You see almost all of it in the movies or on TV. Everybody talks about it. Sometimes it seems as if they never talk about anything else. The whole world seems to be doing it except for you, if you are sixteen years old in a neighborhood like ours. You are the wrong age, too young and too old, just a dirty masturbating kid that nobody wants, not even the whores.

"Let's go back to the neighborhood and get Sadie Cusack," Conny said. "She puts out, man, and that's for sure. That's for damn sure."

There was a girl in the neighborhood—Sadie Cusack—who had a bad reputation so that most of the nice girls, the parochial high school kids, were forbidden to associate with her. I knew her vaguely by sight but I hadn't spoken to her for years.

"She is a pig," I said.

"You got a better proposition?" Conny demanded. "From what I hear she's okay if you don't mind a dirty neck."

"Her neck isn't all that's dirty," I said.

We rode back to Yorkville on the subway and waited until Sadie Cusack emerged from the decomposing tenement where she lived with her family. We persuaded her to walk down to the waterfront with us. She was a fat girl with bad skin and sickly, watery eyes. And she was dirty, as Conny had promised. Pig dirty. In the wintertime when she was going to Julia Richman High School the teachers made her take a bath at least once a week, even if they had to do it themselves in one of the school washrooms. In the summertime I don't think she ever took a bath at all. You could see the dirt mark on her neck like the ring in a bathtub when somebody forgets to wash it out and the dirt and crud dries hard. She was fifteen, younger than we were, but mostly she hung around with guys who were eighteen and nineteen. She was a moron, I suppose, blundering through the general course at Julia Richman over on Second Avenue. The old man was a helpless drunk and the family was always on home relief. There were nine other kids.

We bought sandwiches and a lot of Cokes and took them down to the river with us. We sat on the concrete embankment looking down the river at Welfare Island and the Queensboro Bridge. You could see the cell blocks on the island and it was clear enough so that you could see the convicts walking around. It was hot but not too hot, and there was a breeze from the river that smelt of salt water because the tide was in.

We fed Sadie the sandwiches. She ate like a fat squirrel, gnawing through the bread and meat without ever stopping to taste or swallow the way most people do, just pushing the food into her mouth as if she were feeding a mechanical garbage truck.

"Jesus Christ, Sadie, you'll choke," I said. "Didn't you have any dinner?"

It was nine o'clock in the evening but very light, almost daylight.

"Sure. Canned salmon," said Sadie. "I ate a whole can."

"Out of the can?" Conny said.

"Sure. How else?" she said.

That was the way the Cusacks lived, the kids eating out of tin cans, the old man drunk on the floor or down at Bellevue getting dried out. They were pigs, pig Irish. I shook my head, looking at the prison blocks on Welfare Island, wondering what I was doing here sitting beside this fat pig. She was not the wanton I lusted for. She was not even a respectable whore.

Conny was less particular. He moved in close to Sadie and put an arm around her. Then he squeezed her breast and said, "Sadie's a big girl, McCaffery. She needs plenty of food."

"Take your han' off my tit," said Sadie, reaching for a bottle of Coke.

"Come on, Sadie, don't be like that," said Conny. "We're nice guys. And we got money."

She looked at him contemptuously. "Yeah, you kids," she said. "Where would you get money?"

"Robbing the fast mail," I said. I was bored and irritable. I took out three one-dollar bills and laid them on the concrete, spread out so they made a fan. I put a stone on them to hold them down.

"What do you think I am, a whore?" said Sadie. "You know what you can do with the money. Stick it up your ass."

"It's a dollar too much," I said, wondering precisely how I had violated Sadie's protocol.

"Shut up, McCaffery," Conny said. He put an arm around her again. "Why don't you give us a break?"

"I don't do it no more," said Sadie. She shook her head firmly, just as if she had told him she didn't want, maybe, a cigarette. She wasn't angry or even bothered, but she was firm.

"Ah, come on, don't give us that," said Conny, beginning to be angry with her.

"I don't do it no more," she said. "You think I want to get knocked up? Not by one of you kids anyway. I don't want to get put away in no home for waylaid girls."

"Give us a free show anyway," Conny said. "Come on, be a good kid."

That was what she had been called when we all were little kids: Free Show Sadie. In those days, for a nickel she would let you look, for a dime she would let you touch. Wearily she pulled up her skirts. She had nothing on underneath.

"Come on, spread 'em apart," said Conny.

She obeyed him. He tried to get on top of her and she fought him off with her fists. She rolled away from him, flushed and panting. He had stirred her up. She pulled down her skirt and stared off at the big bridge. She was thinking. You could almost hear the big wooden wheels of her mind turning over slowly. Then she turned to Conny, simple-minded, eager to please.

"I don't do it no more, honest," she said. "But if you give me the three dollars I'll do like I do in the movies."

"What good is that?" said Conny.

"You'll see," she said. "Most of the fellows like it. Anyway, it's all I do now. I told you that. I don't want to get P.G."

Conny argued with her, making various suggestions. She shook her head stubbornly. Her dirty body and slow mind were beginning to disgust me. A flash of rage went through me like electric shock, then the impulse to violence. I wanted to kick Sadie in the way I had kicked the man in the park. I didn't. I picked up the three dollars and handed them to her.

"You can start with Donovan," I said. "And hurry up or you'll be out of a job."

There was one sandwich left. While she was busy with Conny, Sadie kept staring at it. Her gluttony was pathetic. When she was finished she turned to me obediently.

"Skip it," I said. "That I can do for myself, and my hands are cleaner than yours."

"Can I have the sannwich?" she said.

"Eat it!" I said. "For Christ's sake, eat it, you pig. Choke on it if you want to."

"I go down here with all kinds of fellows and nobody talks to me like that," she said.

"So you're not a pig," I said. "You have a figure like Miss America and you take a bath twice a day and soak yourself in Channel No. 5."

She stood up, smoothing her sleazy wrinkled skirt, then wiping her hand on the back of it. For a second I thought she was going to pass up the sandwich out of pride but she couldn't do it. She was a glutton in the same way other people are alcoholics. She picked up the sandwich and gnawed away at it, the three dollars gripped in her left hand.

"Conny, you walk me home," she said. "You brought me down here, you ought to walk me home."

Conny got up, looking sheepish. I knew that he didn't want to be seen with Sadie, but there was nothing he could do.

"Sure, I'll walk you to the corner," he said. "Okay?"

"Not him," said Sadie, looking at me. "Just you."

Conny looked at me and spread his hands: *What can I do?*

"Go ahead, Donovan, she's your girl," I said. "You want my congratulations you got them."

I sat on the concrete embankment after they had gone, watching the dark river and the dark shape of the island. You could see the lights of automobiles crossing the river from both sides. Once it started to get dark it got dark fast, as if somebody had pulled down a curtain.

I was depressed and ashamed of myself because I had been cruel to Sadie the moron. I was sixteen and healthy, but I sat there on the fringe of Yorkville by the East River feeling that I had exhausted all of the reasons for living. The nonexistent pistol was in my right hand. I aimed at my temple and pulled the trigger. It wasn't the lack of a pistol that walled off the yearning for death. It was the knowledge that I had not yet lived.

While my mother lived I had lived through her. There had always been the uncut cord. When she died I had tried to die in my mind, but they had brought me back to life with their dabs of electricity, shot through the dormant brain. Now I sat in the world as a stranger, inhabiting rooms with an enemy.

My mother. I could hardly remember the shape of her face, though I tried, sitting there by the night river. But I could remember the way she had felt when she put her arms around me and I could remember the way she smelled, always of soap and starch. She was as clean as a German nun. It was a mania with her. If she got a spot on her dress, even a little one that didn't show, off came the dress and on went a fresh one.

I got that from her. I like to be clean. My father would sit around in his work clothes, and sometimes when he had stopped for beer he would not bother to change at all but roll into bed in the T shirt he had worn on the scaffold, dropping his work clothes on the floor. I am not like that. I like to be clean. I like to be neat. In the summertime I used to change every day of the week, underwear, shirt, blue jeans, socks, all the way from the skin out.

"She had no right to die," I said to the dark, oily river. "If she hadn't died I'll bet we would have moved away from this crummy neighborhood, away from a place where there are pigs like Sadie Cusack."

Then I thought: Maybe not. The one thing she would never do was to cross the old man's will. She believed what the Church had taught her, and she had been taught to obey her father and then taught to obey her husband. We would never have moved away. She would not have insisted on anything the old man didn't want. She had never refused him. That was why she was dead, because she thought it was her duty to God to give the bull what he wanted.

I felt a wave of sick rage. I stood up with my hands on my hips and spat into the river. I turned away from the river and walked toward home. I knew that Conny would be waiting for me on the corner but I didn't want to see Conny. I didn't want to see anybody except maybe my Aunt Theresa, who wouldn't be home until tomorrow, back from her old maid's vacation at the Carroll Club Camp.

The apartment was empty when I got home, which meant that the old man was standing at the bar in Murphy's or Mallin's, crowded together with people he knew, filling himself with Schaefer's beer until he thought it was cool enough so that he could sleep.

I got into bed quickly. In the dark my mind turned over slowly but precisely like an idling engine. I was thinking of the man we had clouted in the park, wondering what went on in his mind, if that was where it went on. I was curious. He was a good-looking guy, young, with money in his pockets, well-dressed, well-educated. He must have a job, a place where he lived. He must have friends and people he knew, men and women. Why would he want to cruise in the park picking up kids, taking a chance on getting his lumps, maybe even on getting murdered? What was the percentage for him, the P.C.T.?

There was only one conclusion. He wanted to get his lumps. Perhaps he wanted to be beaten to death.

In the day room at the Kips Bay Hospital there had been lots of psychologizing. Patients in a place like that are fascinated by their own condition, a bit in love with their own diseases. That was what they would have said about the man in the park ... that he went to the park in the first place seeking not sex but punishment.

The theory was neat. It made a pattern. But it did not satisfy me that night. I was a Jesuit at heart, unfrocked before I had been ordained but still as stubborn as any Jebby.

Why did I go into the park? I asked myself with my head on the pillow. It wasn't the money. It was something else. I had committed a crime. A clear and deliberate sin. And out of it, almost from the instant Conny and I had boarded the rear end of the crosstown bus, I had derived a sense of life, an awareness that I acted instead of being acted upon.

A clear and deliberate sin. I repeated the words in my mind. A crime against God and man. I had committed a crime of violence. I felt less guilt than I once had felt when I kept my mother waiting for an hour because I had stopped for a Coke with some of the fellows.

I thought of the faggot on the ground, sharp, clear images like those you get in a powerful dream. I could feel again the shock in my legs as I had kicked the helpless body. I wanted to feel guilt as I lay there on my hot pillow. I yearned for it. I felt nothing. It was a patch on my memory, vivid and bright, a few seconds when the blood had flowed full-stream through my body.

Excitement, action, movement, violence. These were the things that made you feel alive, I thought. The old man. He had enjoyed the war. Nowadays he enjoyed the danger that he met each morning when he stepped out onto the high scaffold. He took risks with his own skills and they paid him for it, a hundred and sixty dollars a week.

There was a sound at the door. It was the old man coming in, walking heavily through the parlor, dropping heavily to the bed in his room. A moment before, I had been tired, perfectly happy to lie there on the hot, narrow bed. Now I wanted to go out, to get up and dress and go out into the dangerous city night.

I was afraid, afraid of the bull who sat there now in his undershirt on the edge of his bed filled with beer and good fellowship.

CHAPTER FIVE

I DIDN'T wake up until ten o'clock. The old man had been gone for hours. He drank black tea for his breakfast, making it in an ordinary pan, just throwing a handful of tea leaves into the boiling water, then turning off the fire. It was black and bitter and you couldn't drink it unless the cup was loaded with sugar.

He couldn't stand coffee. It was another thing about him that wasn't quite American even though he was born here. His father drank Irish tea for breakfast, so that was good enough for him. "Coffee rots your guts," he would say. "Tea is the only thing to drink outside of beer and maybe whisky." I argued with him once. "It's what they tan leather with," I told him. "Probably it turns your guts to leather." "Where did you hear a thing like that?" he wanted to know. "In school," I told him. "In chemistry class." He looked at me as if I were crazy and went on drinking his strong black tea.

The tea pan was still on the stove, wet smelly leaves at the bottom. I tossed them into the garbage, rinsed the pan and boiled some water to make myself a cup of instant coffee.

I sat in the parlor drinking my coffee wearing nothing but a pair of shorts. You could tell it was going to be hot, one of those really stinking New York days, hot and humid so that the whole city would reek like one big armpit. We ought to go swimming today, I thought. It is going to be too hot to hang around here.

I finished my coffee and got dressed, then wrapped my swimming trunks in a towel. The house looked like a gypsy camp but I let it go. Old Lady Mulleady was supposed to come in and clean up a little during the day when she got the chance. My Aunt Theresa had fixed that with her before she went on her vacation. Ordinarily Aunt Theresa cleaned up the kitchen and made the beds before she got dressed to go to work down in the Municipal Building in back of the City Hall. She was a clerk in the Marriage License Bureau. Twenty-eight years old, an Irish Catholic virgin, probably hardly even been kissed, and there she stood all day long filling out marriage license forms, looking at people who were getting married.

I slammed the door behind me and went down the stairs fast. Conny was waiting on the corner. I saw that he had his suit and a towel. He looked at me contemptuously and then he laughed.

"Jesus, McCaffery, you sucker," he said. "You know what happened after I left you? I scored. sucker. I scored. Right in her hallway, under the stairs. Not a lousy hand job but the real thing, kid. The real thing."

He made that Italian gesture, snapping his forearm into the air. I could have hit him. I could have knocked him down to the sidewalk and kicked him in the stomach.

"You're a liar." I said.

"So I'm a liar. Who isn't?" he said innocently. "But not about this, kid. Not about this. I'm telling you I banged her right in the hallway."

"You're a liar," I said again.

"Have it your own way," he said agreeably. "You're the one that got skunked."

He wasn't lying. I knew that and I was disgusted with myself because I was jealous, and what guy in his right mind would be jealous because somebody else had scored with a pig like Sadie Cusack? But I was jealous and I hated Conny for having done it. All the way out to Coney Island I kept wondering why she had brushed me off and then let Conny do what he liked. What is wrong with me? I wondered. What in the hell is the matter with me?

The ocean was cool in the morning and very clean, amazingly salt, as always. We swam briskly for half an hour, then cruised along the boardwalk.

"Nothing but Hebes," Conny said benevolently, filled with Irish arrogance.

"Spiritually we are Semites," I said absently. My mind was wandering; the words seemed to form in my mouth without being summoned.

"What?" said Conny.

"In the eyes of God we are all Jews," I said, baiting him now.

"Who says?" Conny demanded.

"Don't blame me," I said. "Blame the Pope. He said it before I did."

"That is a crock," Conny said.

I abandoned the game. Baiting Conny was not worth the effort. The gap between us was too wide. Suddenly I was homesick for school, where at least there were kids with sharp minds and where the Jesuit intelligence seemed to permeate the air of the old corridors. God or no God, at least in school there were minds to oppose. In the neighborhood there was Conny, a dozen Connys.

We went into the ocean again. It was afternoon and by this time the water was like oversalted soup. The beach was crowded and the smell of bodies was carried on the light warm breeze together with the sweetish smell of garbage.

"Let's get out of this," I said. "And next time for Christ's sake let's go to Jones Beach. At least the water there is clean."

On the subway riding home Conny counted his money.

"Three lousy bucks," he said. "Three lousy dollars. How much have you got left?"

"Five," I told him.

"You know what we ought to do tonight?" he said. "We ought to knock off another fag."

The roar of the subway in my ears made me feel as if I were going to explode. It was what I wanted to do. Not just for the money but for the excitement, the sense of danger, and the chance to hurt someone who could not hurt me back.

"It's okay with me," I said.

"You want me to be bait tonight?" Conny said.

"Whatever you say," I told him.

"I think they go more for you," he said. "Vincie McCaffery, the fag's delight."

"Donovan, shut your God damned mouth or I will kick you in the teeth right here in the subway," I said.

"I'm only kidding you, Vince," he said. He put an arm around my shoulders and laughed. "Don't get sore. We're pals, remember? Buddy-buddies."

I calmed down. I let it go. But for a moment I had been mad enough at Conny to have killed him. Buddies, I thought savagely. Buddy-buddies. He's not even a friend of mine. He's like Sadie the pig. He is what I can get.

That night we hung around on the corner until half past ten, then took a bus and rode across the park.

"Let's pick another spot," said Conny. "Not that Joe Chump is going to be back looking for more, but why take a chance?"

We walked uptown for a few blocks along Central Park West. I sat down on a bench just in range of the light from a street lamp. The first time, I had been scared. It had been something new, something unknown. This time I was excited but I wasn't really scared. I was souped up and I felt a kind of exhilaration, the sense that something was going to happen, something violent and conclusive.

I sat on the bench, my mind drifting. I wished I were thirty pounds heavier and tough as a bull, like my old man. Then I wouldn't need Conny with the stupid rock in his stupid hand. Then I could do it all myself, wait until the man was down on his knees, then bring up my own knee hard and at the same instant smash him on the back of the neck with the sharp side of my open hand. I could see the whole thing in my mind, the way I would do it if I had the old man's strength.

I waited in the dark for twenty minutes, half an hour. Three-quarters. There was nothing doing. A few men passed, sauntering, taking it easy. Two of them looked me over and slowed down as they went by but they did not stop. I was almost ready to give up when a man sat down on the bench, close to me.

He wasn't like the first one, who had looked like an ordinary businessman. This one was a genuine queer with dyed hair and pointed shoes and one of those freakish Italian suits. And he came right to the point. When he spoke I felt as if I had been touched with a live wire. The voice was a real queer's voice, high-pitched and effeminate, a woman's voice somehow diseased. Pederast. I didn't know the word that night when I sat on the bench beside the park, but I have learned it since, and when I meet it in print or utter the syllables the word brings up, on the instant, the man of that night and his smell.

"Are you waiting for me, honey?" he said. "Because I'm all ready for you."

He took my hand and squeezed it, sure of himself and arrogant. He reeked with perfume, not cologne or shaving lotion but real perfume, women's perfume with some kind of musk base.

I got control of myself. Stall him a little, I reminded myself. Don't be too eager. Be a little hard to get.

"What's in it for me?" I said.

"For what I give you, darling, you should pay me," he said. "But if you're really nice I'll give you something."

"How much?" I said.

He held up two fingers.

"You know what you can do with the deuce," I said, all of Yorkville in my voice, tough kid, street kid.

"Why, you mercenary little bitch," he said, squeezing my thigh. "All right, then, five. But not until we've had our fun."

"Okay," I said. "For a fin, okay."

He thought I was a commercial kid, a little piece of rough trade. We walked into the park. I had committed only one crime, yet I was a hardened criminal. Donovan had burgled a store and rifled half a dozen parked cars. He had been arrested. But besides me he was an amateur, a juvenile delinquent. My mood was a mood of ice. I was neither juvenile nor delinquent. I was nihilist, criminal and adult, thoroughly dangerous and committed.

It was a matter of moral chemistry. The elements had been in my soul, slumbering like harmless substances in bottles, until all at once they had found the favorable temperature and combined to produce the explosive compound that now was in my brain.

I felt good, thinking as we walked into the park: This one I would like to belt myself. I'd like to break his God damned jaw.

He led the way down the path, then turned into the bushes. There was a place hidden from view by trees on one side, a stone wall on the other. There was no bench. We stood up near the wall. There was a trickle of light from the moon and stars but it was almost dark. I closed my eyes. The perfume was heavy. It was like standing next to a fat woman on the subway, a fat woman loaded with Wool-worth's best. Make believe it's a dame, I said to myself. Make believe it's that fat pig Sadie Cusack.

"Drop your pants, honey," the man whispered. "You precious little darling."

I wanted Conny to come all right, with the big rock in his right hand, and then I didn't want him to come. I was backed against the stone wall and the stone cut into my flesh and I liked it. A part of me liked it and did not want it to stop. There was a sound, a funny noise, like that of an animal having a nightmare, and then I realized that the sound came out of my own mouth.

At just that moment Conny appeared, coming fast out of the bushes. He knew how to handle that rock if he didn't know much else.

"Bastard!" I said. "Son of a bitch!"

I didn't quite know whether I was cursing Conny or myself. I fixed my clothes while Conny went through the man's pockets. Then I stood near the wall, swaying a little, and I vomited. I puked so hard that I thought my stomach was going to come right up through my mouth. I picked up the rock that Conny had used and dropped down beside the guy. He was conscious and trying to talk.

"Don't, boys, please don't," he said.

I smashed the rock into his face, once, twice, three times. I broke his nose, I was sure of that, and smashed his filthy painted mouth.

"Quit it, for Christ's sake," Conny said. "We've got the dough, let's get out of here."

"Shut up, Donovan," I said. "This is half the God damned fun."

Conny backed away from me. He was frightened of me in the way people are frightened of lunatics and wild men. But I was not afraid of myself.

"Jesus, McCaffery, you're crazy," Conny said. He crossed himself quickly in the starlight as if to ward off the evil eye.

"So I'm crazy," I said.

I stood up and kicked the man in the stomach, sorry that I was wearing sneakers and could not break his ribs. I wished I had been wearing combat boots, the boots of a parachute infantryman, steel-tipped and lethal. I wanted to kill the man on the ground, to smash him to bits, to cut him up into little pieces and put him into the garbage.

Conny grabbed my arm. "Let go," he said. "Do you want to wait for a cop, maybe? You're nuts, McCaffery. You are off your rocker."

"So is that your business?" I said.

We walked out of the park slowly. Under a street light we stopped.

"Jesus, there's blood on your hand," said Conny.

I looked at my right hand, the one that had held the rock. There was blood on my wrist and fingers. I licked it off, then spat into the gutter. The man's perfume clung to me and the smell of it made me sick.

"The dirty bastard. I should have killed him," I said.

"For rolling a fag you don't get much even if you get caught," said Conny. "Killing people is different. And even fags are people."

"How much did we get?" I asked.

Conny was counting the money.

"Sixty-three bucks," he said. "Brand new money, fresh from the mint."

"How long did it take us?"

Conny looked at the cheap watch on his wrist and said, "An hour and fifteen minutes altogether."

"That's good money," I said. "That's almost a buck a minute, do you know that?"

I was thinking of the old man and his four and a half an hour that he earned up high on a scaffold with a trowel and a mortarboard in his hand. Screw him, I thought. Him and his four and a half an hour. I thought of him, standing big in his undershirt, peeling bills off the roll from his pocket, handing them to me as if he were king. I wished I could tell him on Saturday night that he knew what he could do with his money.

We threw the wallet into a sewer and rode back to our own neighborhood. When we got off the bus I could still smell the perfume. It was on my skin and in my mouth and nostrils. I needed something to make it go away.

"I could drink a can of beer," I said. "Maybe even two cans."

"How are we going to get beer?" Conny wanted to know. "The cops have been raising hell with the delicatessens. As for the bars, you might as well ask for heroin as to ask for beer unless you got a draft card or a driver's license to prove you are eighteen."

"There are ways and ways," I told him.

"So name one."

"Your old man gets his beer from Schultz's, right?" I said.

"Schultz won't give it to me," said Conny.

"So you call Schultz from the booth in the candy store and tell him to send six cans of beer to the house," I said.

"So?"

"So we meet the kid in front of your house, give him the money and take the beer," I explained.

Schultz's delivery boy was a bright-faced Puerto Rican kid with a flashing smile, eager to please as a puppy. And he didn't care who got the beer as long as he got the money and didn't have to climb the five flights of stairs to the Donovan trap on the top floor. It worked like a charm. We carried the beer down to the river and sat on the embankment in the same place we had sat with Sadie Cusack. A cool breath rose from the river. I speared a beer can with the opener that was in the bag and filled my mouth with the cold beer, sloshing it around like mouthwash, letting the bitter beer taste get rid of the taste of the queer. Then I swallowed the beer and took another swig. Conny was working on his can.

"Like pouring it down a rathole," I said. "To quote an eminent authority on the subject of Schaefer's beer."

Conny looked at me curiously.

"Sometimes I don't understand you," he said. "Why did you want to clout the guy after I had knocked him cold? I told you, you might have killed him."

"I should have killed him," I said.

Conny shook his head. "It's only a way of getting some dough," he said. "You shouldn't let yourself get personal about it."

"We got the money, didn't we?" I said. "I felt like clouting the guy. What are you bitching about?"

"My brother Al told me—"

"Screw your brother Al," I said. "Does he know everything? Is he God?"

"He knows," said Conny. "He knows a lot."

That was the difference between Conny and me. For Conny it was just a way of getting some money, safer than trying to snatch purses or rob a store. For me it was something different right from the beginning.

I could feel the beer when I had finished the first can and I could smell it too, and the smell blanked out the stink of the perfume that was on my skin. I was fairly used to beer. Cops or no cops we all drank it when we could get it. I started the third can, then remembered that my aunt would be home when I got there. She was sure to smell the beer on my breath if I got close to her. The old man didn't worry me. The first thing he did when he entered the house was to head for the refrigerator and a can of cold Schaefer's. If you have been drinking beer you can't smell it on somebody else. But my Aunt Theresa didn't drink, except for a glass of wine at Christmas. She was sure to smell it and then I would have to sit through a lecture.

The only thing to do, I decided, was to stay out late enough so that she would be asleep when I got home. We sat on the bank of the river and finished the beer. I felt good. A little dizzy from the beer, but good. My share of the money was tucked into the little pocket under my belt and I touched the bump it made with my fingertips. It is a funny thing: I knew I had stolen the money but I felt as though I had earned it, just as much as if I'd earned it peddling papers or even laying bricks on the high scaffold.

We hung around the neighborhood until midnight, then Conny took off. I stayed on the streets until after one in the morning, walking back and forth on 86th Street, passing the honky-tonks and the beer joints. It was like the midway of a traveling carnival. The service police, always in pairs, wearing starched summer clothes, cruised past the beery joints, looking into the ones that were marked: Off Limits to Service Personnel. They were worse than real cops, never cracking a smile, hardly speaking to one another. I remember thinking, looking at them, I hope I never get drafted.

Still, on that street there was a raw sense of life, brightly lighted and noisy, an awareness of people crowded together in the embrace of companionship. It was poorman's gaiety but I was envious just the same. It was the music that did it, the brassy music that came through the doors into the hot street. That and the beer in my blood. I was lonely. I envied even the soldiers and sailors who moved along in twos and threes, locked together in a conspiracy of comradeship. I envied the careless laughs of the girls, high-pitched and reckless. I even envied the slabfaced service police who walked with the cadence of prison guards but who were always together, always in pairs, identically dressed, blood brothers.

At half past one I went home. I was quiet as a sneak thief coming into the house but my aunt heard me. She must have been waiting up for me.

"Vincent," she called. "Come in and say hello to your aunt."

I stood in the doorway of her room, not wanting to get closer to her because of the beer on my breath. She was in bed with the pillow propped up behind her, a *Catholic Digest* on her lap. I hung back but she held out her arms and there was nothing I could do. I kissed her cheek and she hugged me. If she did notice the beer on my breath she didn't say anything about it. I had walked the streets alone for nothing.

She smiled at me and patted the bed. I sat down beside her. She had a two-week vacation tan and her black hair was brushed and shiny. She looked nice, but to me, then, she still looked like an Irish old maid.

She was my mother's kid sister and she came to live with us when my mother first got sick and had to have someone to help out. After my mother died she stayed on in the house, cooking our dinner, making the beds, getting our breakfast for us before she went off to her own work. She was really an unpaid servant though that didn't occur to me during the years she lived with us. She was simply my mother's sister, my Aunt Theresa.

She was pretty and small like my mother but without my mother's real beauty. She had the same dark hair and the same clear blue eyes, the color of clean-washed denim. Under her cotton nightgown I could see her breasts, small and hard-looking as apples. She was a virgin. I knew that. I was as certain of that as I was that the sun would come up in the morning. There was something about her that made you think of a young nun—a calm, innocent quality.

"Vincent, it's almost two o'clock," she said mildly. "You shouldn't be on the streets so late."

"I was with Donovan," I told her. "We went to the show."

"I'll bet you haven't had a decent meal all the time I've been gone," she said. "I shouldn't have left you alone."

"I ate enough," I said. "I'm not a kid. I'm almost seventeen."

I sat on the edge of her bed holding her hand, wondering what she would say if I told her what Conny and I had been doing earlier in the park.

She wouldn't believe me, I thought. If I swore it was true on my mother's grave still she would not believe it. She would think I was crazy, that the illness had returned, or that it was the Devil in me making me say crazy things. She was simple-minded. She was a grown woman with a job downtown and she had lived in New York City all of her life and still she was as simple-minded as a Connemara peasant. There were things I knew just from hanging around the neighborhood, things I knew about people and what they could do to one another, that my Aunt Theresa knew nothing about. I had picked up more out of the air just inhaling and exhaling than she had learned in ten years of working in the Municipal Building. And if you had taken her by the hand and showed her things, forced her to peep through a thousand keyholes, she would not have believed her own eyes.

Still, I liked her. Mostly, I suppose, because she loved me in her simple-minded way but partly because she was my mother's sister and my own flesh and blood. The old man. Well, I knew that he was my father. Sometimes I could see it when I looked in the mirror. But I did not think of him then as my own flesh and blood. Fiercely my soul insisted that it was only an accident that he was my father, a piece of bad luck. Aunt Theresa was different. Looking at her propped up against the white pillow was a little like looking at my mother. Or perhaps like looking at a bad photograph of my mother. But the resemblance was strong enough to mean something to me.

"Don't forget to say your prayers," she told me, kissing my hand. "Good night now, Vincent. Sweet dreams."

I kissed her good night and went to my room. In the little drawer of my work table was a rosary that had belonged to my mother. I took it out and sat on the edge of the bed with the beads in my hand. I looked at the crucifix—it was solid silver, then at the beads, and then I began to count: eenie, meenie, minie, moe, catch a nigger by the toe.

It was just as good as the Hail Mary, just as good as the Our Father. By that time that summer my unbelief was hardening. I did not believe in God, yet in the same breath I hated him. I fought with myself, arguing that to hate God was to admit his power, but the arguments hung fire. That summer I went on thinking that God was a phony and a fake but still the louse who screwed things up.

That summer, if I had believed in anything I would have believed for preference in the Devil. But I didn't. I was simply acting out a kind of demonian calendar. I wanted to believe in myself, to demonstrate to myself the fact that I was alive and not just walking through the world inhaling and exhaling, eating and shitting. I wanted to be engaged with life, not merely to be alive.

I sat on the bed with the beads in my hand, saying the eenie, meenie, minie, moe. What the hell! I thought. I said the Hail Mary, just for the fun of it and because I could say it in beautiful Latin and I liked the sound of the Latin words.

"... *ora pro nobis peccatoribus, nunc et in hora mortis nostrae. ... Sancta Maria!*"

I dropped the beads back into the drawer and got into bed. The beer I had drunk by the river bank had almost worn off and my mouth felt dry. I wanted another can of beer and I knew there was plenty in the kitchen but for a long time I lay there, afraid I would wake one of them if I went to the refrigerator. Finally I took a chance. There were eight cans of Schaefer's, neat as soldiers in a line, stowed in the rack on the refrigerator door, a little bead of sweat on the tin. This was something I had never done before but tonight I had thought it out. He always had two or three cans when he came home and I knew the way his mind worked. He would never count what was left. He would know more or less that there were seven—eight cans. If I took, say, three, he would notice that. One he would never miss.

I speared the can, put the opener away and carried the beer to my bedroom. I lay on the bed sucking the can, staring at the airshaft window. That window is like my life, I thought. It gives you a view of nothing, it lets in no light, admits no air.

I had something. My unbelief. Sometimes it was a positive thing that filled me with pride and with contempt for others.

Probably I was slightly drunk. I lay in the dark thinking of Conny. I would have been willing to bet money that Conny was awake right now, worrying about what to say at confession, scared that the priest would tell him to go to the cops and scared not to tell the priest for fear he might die in mortal sin and go straight down to the bowels of hell.

I wasn't worried about that.

I went to confession often enough so that I would not attract attention. Bless me father for I have sinned. Lascivious thought. I looked at a girl's legs on the subway. I told a lie to my aunt. Make a good Act of Contrition. Ten Hail Marys. I thought of the words of "The Croppy Boy," a song I had heard my father sing:

The robes were off and in scarlet there stood a yeoman captain with fiery glare. With fiery glare and with fury hoarse, instead of a blessing he breathed a curse.

I cursed in the hot night.

If God made me then who made God?

My mind attacked the impregnable circle, wanting to construct a square that I could measure and tear apart. I had no right to my unbelief. I could not prove it. Yet I wanted to possess it even if I had to invent the rhetoric.

CHAPTER SIX

WENT to confession. I went to Mass. I even took Communion. And I went on jackrolling in Central Park whenever Conny and I needed money, and sometimes even when we had plenty of money in our pockets just for the hell of it, for something to do.

Then one night things went wrong. Just as Conny's rock came down two cops came out of the bushes, night sticks in the air. The pale light glittered on their shields and the brass buttons of their summer shirts.

"All right, you two, up against the wall. Hands in the air."

We leaned against the wall, hands up, while one of the cops searched us quickly. I had sixty dollars in the little pocket of my jeans. Conny had about forty. Outside of the money we were clean. No knives. No zip guns. No stockings loaded with sand. We were intelligent Irish-Americans, too smart for that kind of Puerto Rican crap.

The second cop helped the man to his feet. He wasn't badly hurt. There was a cut on the back of his head where Conny had hit him with the rock but it didn't amount to much. He was a man in his early forties, scared and very agitated.

"This is all a mistake," he said, touching his head with the tips of his fingers. "It's all a misunderstanding."

"Yeah, yeah," said one of the cops. "We know what kind of misunderstanding. Suppose we all go to the station house and straighten things out."

He was a slim, mean-looking cop, very neat, wearing a shirt that must have been tailored for him by hand. The other cop was big and beefy.

"It's all a mistake," the man repeated. "There's no need to make any trouble."

The thin cop moved close to him.

"Look, mister," he said, "somebody is wrong in this setup. Do you want me to put you under arrest for soliciting these kids?"

The man shrugged helplessly.

"Let's go," said the thin cop. "Come on, you two. Move. In front of us."

He prodded us with the tip of his club, moving us out of the park, Conny and myself leading the way, the two cops behind us with the man between them still trying to explain to them that the whole thing was a mistake.

A police car stood at the curb. They loaded the three of us into the back and cut out toward the station house with the siren wide open. People stopped in the street to stare.

It is a dirty neighborhood once you are a block west of the park ... Puerto Ricans, colored people, all on the sidewalks in front of the run-down brownstone houses that have been turned into rooming houses. There are a few cheap hotels and a few Spanish bars but mostly it is dreary and drab except for the people on the streets with their portable radios going full blast, the P.R. girls in their bright-colored skirts and their long hair black as silk, the colored men like statues.

The police station was older and dirtier than St. J————'s Church in Yorkville. We stood in front of the sergeant's desk. There was that cop smell that you always get in a station house or any place that cops hang out. The sergeant was a man of fifty with white hair cut short like a soldier's and a long, lean, leathery face—an old-timer, not one of those young cops who go to law school and study psychology and sociology in courses at City College. He had eyes like sharp gray knives.

"What have you got?" he asked, looking down at us like a judge from the high desk.

"Jackrollers," said the thin cop. "We caught them right in the act."

"Did they get his money?" the sergeant asked.

"They didn't have time," the cop explained. "But they clouted the guy. We saw that."

"Assault with attempt to commit robbery," the sergeant said. He wrote something on his pad.

"This is all a mistake," the man said. "This is all a misunderstanding."

In the yellow police-station light I got a good look at the man. Everything about him spoke of money, real money. He was straight-backed, dressed in a good gray suit with a raw-silk shirt and a heavy black silk tie. His hair was gray at the temples and his long, lean face was healthy with tan. He suggested yachts and expensive beaches. In his hand was a very large, very white handkerchief with bloodstains on it from his head. He had a cultivated voice, nothing effeminate about it, the voice of an actor or perhaps a college professor. His voice and his manner reminded me of one of the Jesuits at school, a priest who came from a rich family and who had been to Harvard College before he went to the seminary.

"Now, you sit down on the bench over there for a few minutes," the sergeant told him. "We'll take care of you right away."

"But it's all a mistake," the man insisted.

"Just sit down," the sergeant said respectfully but in a way that meant you shouldn't argue. He turned to us. "All right, you two." He pointed at me. "What's your name?"

"Vincent Michael Joseph McCaffery," I said, without any hesitation. In advance Conny and I had decided to play innocent if we were caught, so there was no sense in trying to give a phony name.

"Address?" the sergeant said.

I gave him the address.

"Age?"

"Sixteen."

I gave straight answers to all the questions and Conny did the same. The sergeant wrote it all down, not on the blotter but on a plain pad. Then he said, "What are you doing on the West Side?"

"We went for a walk," I said.

"What were you doing in the park?"

"It's cooler there," said Conny.

"It's a public place," I said.

"And how did you meet this gentleman?" He pointed at the man who was sitting on a bench on the other side of the room.

"He spoke to me," I said. "He wanted to show me a place in the park. Shakespeare's Garden."

"And why did you hit him?"

"We didn't hit him," Conny said. "We pushed him and he fell down. I guess that's when he hurt his head."

"Why did you push him?"

"We were defending our honor," I said.

The sergeant laughed. "Where did you get a line like that?" he said. He looked at the thin cop. "Did you see Donovan hit him?" he said. "Did you see McCaffery hit him?"

"Not exactly," the cop explained. "It was dark. He was on the ground when we moved in. But they hit him, all right. Who else could have hit him?"

"Maybe he just got tired and fell down by himself," the sergeant said. He picked up Conny's money, then mine, counted it, then put it down. "Two sixteen-year-old kids from Yorkville with a hundred bucks between you. Times must have changed since I was a kid. Do you work for a living, either of you?"

"Not exactly," I said. "We get an allowance."

"So where did you get the money?"

"We hit a crap game," said Conny.

"For a hundred bucks? A kid's crap game?" said the sergeant. "Don't try to con me or I'll break your little Irish skulls."

"We were lucky," Conny said.

"Your luck can change," the sergeant said. "You can orap out just like that." He snapped his fingers.

"Sergeant, if you please!"

It was the man Conny had clouted. He had his self-confidence back. Now he was a citizen standing on his rights. The voice was the voice of a rich man used to being obeyed at once.

"Yes, sir?" the sergeant said.

"Why are you keeping me here?" said the man. "I have not made a complaint. I am not going to make a complaint."

"What is your name?" the sergeant asked.

"Howard Smith."

"Well, listen to me, Mr. Smith," the sergeant said in a kind of patient voice as if he were talking to a child. "These two hoodlums tried to rob you. If they had hit you a little harder they might have killed you. Do you mean to tell me you don't want to make a complaint?"

"It was all a mistake," the man said. "I touched the tall dark boy, McCaffery, innocently enough, but he misunderstood and pushed me. I fell and hurt my head. That is all there was to it."

The sergeant sighed wearily. "All right, you can go," he said.

When the man had gone Conny laughed and nudged me in the ribs.

"Shut up," the sergeant told him.

We stood there in front of the desk.

"You want to hold them on suspicion?" the sergeant said.

The cops hesitated. If they held us on their own they would have to show up in court tomorrow, on their off-time, and the chances were it would be all for nothing with no real complaining witness.

"What's the use?" said the thin cop. "The next time, we'll make it stick."

The cops went back to their patrol. We heard the car's motor roar as they pulled away from the station house. The sergeant looked down at us.

"Now, you kids listen to me," he said. "This is a tough neighborhood, tougher than where you come from. We got trouble enough over here without you kids from the East Side sticking your nose in it. If we pull you in again we'll lock you up just on general principles, and your parents will have to come over here to get you out. That way at least you'll get your ass beat off. Now, go on home. Get out of here and go home and stay away from the West Side."

"Yes, sir," we said together.

He handed us our money and we went into the street. It was a long dark street lined with filthy brownstone houses. One street light was out, the other one looked as if it were dying. There was garbage in the gutters even near the police station. We walked away from the station house steadily but not too fast, not saying anything and keeping close to the curb, away from the little front basements which were like dark little caves, places where a P.R. with a knife could hide so that you'd never see him until he had the knife at your throat. When we reached the edge of the park we stopped. We both lit cigarettes.

"I told you," Conny said. "It's just like my brother Al explained. They don't have the nerve to make a complaint."

He was all big shot, brushing it off, but his hand was trembling just the same when he brought the cigarette up to his mouth. The fear of the cops had touched him; he was no real rebel, but only a thief.

We caught the bus and rode back to York Avenue. On the corner we stood by ourselves outside the food shop. There was a red neon sign overhead and it flashed on Conny's devastated face, on and off, on and off. I could see that he was scared, a scared kid.

"So we're out of business," Conny said.

"Who says so?" I asked.

"You heard what the cop said," said Conny. "If they pick us up again they'll make the old man come and get us. I don't know about your old man, but if mine had to haul his ass over there to get me he would take it out in trade."

Conny was finished. I could see that. The smell of the police station had finished him. Donovan the big shot, with his brother Al and his big rock. Even if I could talk him into working the racket again he would be no good at it.

"So you're out of business," I said. "Me, I need the money."

"You're crazy," said Conny. "You can't work it alone."

"Screw, Donovan, you bore me," I said.

I stood on the corner all by myself, the sick red light in my face. I was disgusted. I had been fed up with Conny and I was glad to be rid of him, but I was used to the excitement and the sense of danger. I couldn't see how I was going to get the same kicks out of anything else.

CHAPTER SEVEN

Two nights later I stood on the corner alone, my hands in my pockets, nothing to do and nowhere to go. It was early evening, a balmy night of the kind that offers New Yorkers hope that they will actually survive the summer. The air seemed clean and fresh after a week of muggy weather. I had eaten dinner with my aunt, then changed into crisp chino trousers and a fresh white T shirt. I stood teetering on the balls of my feet, sniffing the promising, expectant air.

A long white Cadillac pulled into the curb and stood there, throbbing away like a big sleek animal. There was nobody in it but the driver, a dark man in a white suit. He was looking me over. I could feel his eyes fixed on me and it made me uncomfortable. I stared back at him, then said, tough kid, street kid, "What's the matter, mister, do I owe you any money?"

He laughed at me. "Are you Vincent McCaffery?" he asked.

I crossed the sidewalk and stood beside the car. "I don't know you," I said. "How do you know me?"

"I knew your name and your address," said the man. "And I asked some kids on another corner where I could find you. A tall kid with bad skin told me to try this corner."

Donovan, I thought. Conny. My buddy-buddy.

"What do you want with me?" I asked, looking at the long rich car.

"I want to talk to you," said the man. "Come on for a ride."

I hesitated. The man smiled at me. "Come on, don't be afraid," he said. "What can you lose by some conversation?"

It was the car that got me. I had never been inside a Cadillac before, and this one was a beautiful job, brand new and half a block long. I figured: What *can* I lose? I was bored and disgusted. I got into the car. There was a smell of new leather. The man stepped on the gas and we rolled away from the curb. The car was smooth, as smooth as silk. You could hardly hear the motor but you could feel all the power purring away like a big cat.

We rode west and cut into Central Park at 86th Street. Until we were on the park crossdrive the man did not say a word. When we were in the sunken drive, he offered me a cigarette and said, "The cops let you go, huh?"

The voice was soft and not New York; the man's hands on the wheel were steady.

"They had nothing on us," I said, still the street-corner tough, wondering how the man knew I had been in the station house and what his angle was.

He braked to a stop for a red light and laughed, then said very easily, "I'm on your side, boy. I know what happened the other night."

"What are you, psychic?" I asked.

"I know all about it," the man said. "The guy you clouted was a client of mine. He gave me your name and address."

A clot of fear formed in my chest. Maybe the guy who had refused to make a complaint in the police station had his own way of handling things. I glanced at the man beside me, estimating my chances, then said, "So what do you want from me?"

"Maybe nothing," the man said. "But what you did, it's not smart." He turned south on Central Park West. He handled the big car as if it had been a baby carriage, smooth, easy-driving, precision but no effort. "It's not smart," he repeated when we were headed south. "Some night you will run into a guy who is able to defend himself. A guy can be queer and tough too, you know. I knew a lightweight contender who was queer as a three-dollar bill. Or you might run into a queer who packs a gun or a knife. You might be dead some night if you go on jackrolling faggots in Central Park."

"Thanks for the advice," I said. "What are you, a social worker? Since when did the Youth Board start to hand out Cadillacs?"

He wasn't annoyed by the needling. "I'm a businessman," he said. "I've got a business proposition for you."

"So make your pitch," I said.

"Drop the Dead End kid stuff," said the man. "It's not becoming. And ride down to my place with me. We can talk better there."

There was something about the man beside me that fascinated me and held me in that car. It wasn't just the big car. It was the man himself. He was on the wrong side of the law, I could feel that. He was dangerous as a rattlesnake. But he was different from the cheap hoodlums I knew by sight in the neighborhood, dumb criminals like Donovan's brother who was sitting in a cell up the river doing two-and-a-half to five. Whatever he was, this man, he was of the first class. I felt that from the beginning. And I wasn't afraid. I had the feeling that here was destiny, offering to fill in the blank space for me.

"Where are we going?" I said.

"To the Village," the man said. "I own a house down there."

We drove along Seventh Avenue, the garment district, dark and locked up for the night, a sense of exhaustion on the dirty littered streets. Here and there high up in the buildings were wedges of melon-colored light where people worked in desperation or old night cleaners toiled. The district was a madhouse in the daytime but at night it was forlorn as the moon.

We cut into the narrow streets of Greenwich Village, making a number of abrupt turns, finally pulling up in front of a house on a quiet street that had trees on both sides. It was a red brick house, maybe twenty-four feet wide, white shutters at the windows, a brass knocker on the door, which was painted dark red. There was a brass plaque set into the brick wall beside the door: Waverly Nursing Home.

We entered the house. Just inside the door was a bare lobby with a nurse in a white uniform sitting behind a reception desk. That was as far as the gag went. The rest of the house went with the car. The whole place was air-conditioned. There were deep rugs and pictures on the walls. A colored maid in a gray uniform opened the inside door.

"Bring us some cold beer, Mamie, in my office," said the man, giving her his Panama hat.

His office was on the street floor in the back of the house, a big room with a bow window hung with deep-red curtains. There was half an acre of polished desk, three telephones, different colors, three or four club chairs in red leather, real leather, soft as butter, soft to sit on as a bed.

"You drink beer, kid?" the man said.

"Whenever I can get it," I said.

The maid brought in a tray with four bottles of Danish beer and two tall polished glasses. We watched her pour the beer carefully as a chemist. When she had gone the man looked at me shrewdly, then handed me a glass of beer. He sat at his desk behind a lamp with a green shade and I studied him. For the first time since he had picked me up I realized that he was a colored guy, not black the way some of them are but a light coffee color, a good-looking man with strong black hair. He was very clean, as if he took a shower three or four times a day. His white suit was made of silk and even then, before I knew much about things like that, I understood that it was tailor-made and not by the tailor around the corner. It fitted him in the way that suits are fitted to movie actors, easy in the shoulders but flat, not a wrinkle anywhere. His voice was low and rich, the words flowing easily. It wasn't a colored man's accent but a voice that was softer than what you hear on the streets of New York City.

"I'm not running a con game, boy," he said. "The reason you're here is that the guy you clouted, Mr. Smith, was impressed with you. Impressed enough to remember your name and your address."

"Is he one of those queers who likes to be clouted?" I asked, remembering the amateur psychiatrists at the Kips Bay Hospital.

The man laughed. "Only sometimes," he said. "And I've tried to persuade him to stay away from Central Park. Right now he's in Hollywood, but he'll be back, boy. He'll be back."

I sipped the beer, thinking, I like this guy, this colored guy. He is graceful and easy and he doesn't give a damn, but underneath you can feel the hardness. He was not a man to fool with. You felt that in the same way that you felt his charm.

"My name is Lawrence Johnson. It's my real name," he said. "They call me Easy Tiger. Tiger because I'm mean when you cross me. Easy because I'm easy to get along with otherwise. I'm a supplier. In plain language, a pimp. But I'm not just a fancy man with a couple of hustlers on the string. I'm a businessman. I own this house, all of it. I don't owe a dime of mortgage money. I own that car, the Caddie, and I've got a Jag, an open job, that I use in the country. And I've got friends. On the police force, and higher up than that. A lot higher up than that."

I tasted the beer again. It was smoother than canned beer and had more body to it. I felt a little thrill of danger. I understood that this was fate. I had volition. I could get up, put the glass of beer on the tray, walk out of the air-cooled house into the hot summer's night, return to the corner in Yorkville where I had been standing less than an hour ago. My will was free. I was not an object. I knew that if I stayed here in this room it would be because I had made a deliberate choice.

I made the choice. I sat in the soft leather chair and held the thin glass in my hand, looking at my host, the Tiger.

He laughed quietly and shook his head. "Jackrolling in Central Park. A good-looking kid like you," he said. "That is for suckers. Dumb Puerto Rican kids who can only get by in the dark. A kid like you, good-looking, nice voice, intelligent, you could make a fortune out of the fags without taking any chances by hanging around the park at night where you might get your head blown off by a cop."

"How?" I said.

"You've got something to sell. Sell it," said the Tiger. "That way it's a business transaction. Nobody gets hurt. Nobody gets arrested. And you get paid. But good."

"What do you think I am?" I said. "I'm no fruit player. I'm no lousy queer."

"Keep your shirt on," the Tiger said. "Anyway, everybody is a little queer. But that's not the point. The point is, give them what they want. Nothing rough. Nothing dangerous. Nothing you won't like, if you get what I mean." He looked at me steadily, then said. "Tell me the truth, now. Have you ever been with a queer? All the way, I mean?"

"What do you think I am?" I said again, slow red anger touching the back of my neck.

The Tiger laughed. "What do I think you are?" he said. "I think you are a kid who is looking for action and doesn't know where to find it. Hanging around the street corner. Drinking beer from a can in an alley. Moving around in the balcony of some third-run picture house hoping you'll pick up some married woman who will take you home for a roll in the hay. And not finding anything. Not anything at all."

He had me pinned and pegged, the way you pin down a moth in the biology lab. It made me uncomfortable and I turned red in the face. The Tiger leaned forward, his arms on the big polished desk, left hand ornamented with one of those big officer's rings with a stone in the middle. I could read the words on it: Fort Benning.

"You tell me the truth now, Vincent," he said. "Have you ever been with a woman? I don't mean wriggling around in some alley or fooling around in the back of the show. I mean in a bed with clean sheets on it and a girl who really knows the score."

"Not exactly," I said. "No."

If another person had asked the question I would have lied, made up half a dozen stories, offered to fight if I was doubted. But this colored man, the Easy Tiger, seemed from the first to have my number. I knew without thinking about it that there was no use in trying to lie to the Tiger because somehow the Tiger seemed to understand exactly what was going on in my mind.

"Not exactly," he said. "But you'd like it, wouldn't you? You lie awake nights thinking about it. And you wonder what's the matter with you and why you still haven't scored that home run."

I didn't say anything. I finished the beer in my glass and the Tiger opened another bottle. I could feel the beer. It was stronger than the Schaefer's I was used to. My lips were pleasantly numb and I had a sense of high confidence. I felt good. And I felt at home in that big rich room. I felt as if I belonged there, even in my chinos and T shirt.

"One thing, kid," the Tiger said. "I'm a pimp but I'm not a son of a bitch. How about your folks? How about your mother, for instance?"

"My mother is dead," I said promptly. I felt no flash of guilt. I felt nothing. I simply made the flat announcement. Even today as the scene races through my mind, each detail and trick of speech clear, this fact amazes me. I sat in the Tiger's red chair and uttered my mother's name and she did not offer to rescue me.

"What about the old man?" the Tiger said.

"I hate him," I said. "And he doesn't care whether I live and breathe or not. He wouldn't even get me a job."

The Tiger filled my glass. "Figures," he said. "A kid with a happy, happy home life wouldn't be clobbering people in the park." He looked at me steadily again, then said, "I can get you a job maybe. But before that you can find out what it's all about right here in this house. Not next week. Not tomorrow. But right now."

"I thought you did business with queers," I said, all at once on my guard.

"I do business in sex," the Tiger said. "All kinds, every kind. If a guy wanted to sleep with a sheep I would go out and find him a broad-minded sheep. For a price." He laughed. "That hasn't come up yet," he said. "But it's about the only thing that hasn't. We get men here looking for men. And we get men here looking for women. And brother, let me tell you, we get women here look-ing for kids just like you. Why do you think I took the trouble to drive up to Yorkville to get you? I've got customers, Vincent, people with money, and I can't put an ad in the paper for help."

I sat back in the big leather chair and closed my eyes. The beer was working. And the things the Tiger had been saying, they were working too. I touched the arms of the chair, feeling the soft red leather. It felt almost like human skin. From somewhere in another part of the house came the sound of music. Then I heard a girl laugh, a high-pitched sexy laugh.

Eyes closed, I listened to the music, sweet jazz from a long way off. I had the sensation you get sometimes when you wake up from a vivid dream. Things were at the same time real and intensely unreal. There was suspension of disbelief. I was both actor and observer. I felt that strongly: the sensation that I was watching myself, hearing myself. Almost from the instant I had stepped into the Tiger's white Cadillac I had felt that I was acting a part in a sharp, grotesque play. I was the thespian somnambulist. The part was there, written for me by someone who understood me better than I understood myself. All I had to do was walk through the action and utter the lines.

"Come on upstairs and I'll show you something," the Tiger said. "Forget the beer. You can have something better than beer later on if you want it."

We went into a carpeted hall, then up a narrow flight of stairs, then down another hall to a small room at the back of the house. There were pictures on the walls, prints, but such good ones I thought they were paintings. The Tiger took a picture from the wall. There was a peephole behind it, a one-way vision arrangement, mirror-backed, of the kind that is put on apartment house doors. The Tiger looked through the hole and smiled.

"Take a look," he said.

I put my eye to the peephole. There was a man on a bed being entertained by two girls. He was middle-aged, with a pot belly, gray hair, and neglected, spindly legs. The girls were kids of my age, maybe a little older, and good-looking, one of them a small blonde, the other a dark hispanic type. It was the first time in my life that I had seen a naked woman in full light except for my aunt once, and by accident, when I had opened the bathroom door. I was fascinated and faintly ill. Then I became more detached. I had the sensation you might have if you were witness to someone's execution in the electric chair. The two little whores had the man at their mercy. They played upon his febrile passion in the way a good jazz pianist will improvise on the keyboard. Innocent, ignorant as I was, I understood that what I saw was a man enslaved and degraded by his own nature. It was not a pretty sight, but it had a sharp, acidulous educational value.

The Tiger laughed quietly and closed the peephole. He replaced the picture and straightened it carefully. He was neat and everything in the house was neat.

"Do you know what he's paying for that party?" he asked. "Two hundred dollars, plus room and liquor. Those are hundred-dollar girls and we don't give a discount for quantity."

"How much do the girls get?" I asked.

"They get half," the Tiger said. "I'm a businessman, an agent. I'm not a crook."

I turned my face toward the wall between the two rooms. As if through the lath and plaster, in my mind's eye, I could see the scene that was being enacted behind that wall.

"Why does he do it?" I asked the Tiger. "Why would he pay that kind of money to be made a fool of?"

"Because he has lost the ability to taste," the Tiger said. "He can't feel anything or taste anything—himself or his wife or his children, his job or the ordinary girl he might knock off. His whole life has lost its taste and he is trying to get it back. He is trying to taste something, to feel something, even if it's only for a few seconds."

"Will he feel it?" I asked.

The Tiger shrugged and said, "Who knows? Who cares?"

We stood in the little room. The Tiger put a hand on my shoulder. He was a pimp, a Negro pimp, outside the law and paying off. He was a criminal and he could be vicious. These things I understood. But I liked him. I responded to him. He spoke to my condition. He does not speak to my condition now, but I cannot find any hatred for him in my heart.

"How about it, kid?" he said. "Do you want to meet one of my young ladies?"

I could not speak because my mouth was dry with fear. I nodded, and the Tiger led the way down the hall to a big bedroom like the one we had watched through the peephole. The walls were painted a dark color, brown or purple, it was hard to tell which in the dim light. There was only one light, from a little lamp beside the bed. There was heavy carpeting wall to wall, and near the bed over the carpet was a white fur rug. The bed was big and it had just been made up with crisp fresh sheets that had been turned down. There were comfortable chairs with tables beside them and near the windows stood a dark-red chaise longue.

Sometimes in the neighborhood we had talked about whores and whorehouses. I always thought of a dirty place in a ruined tenement building that stank of dog piss and old beer, with sagging beds and filthy sheets soiled with a thousand copulations. I could imagine my old man going into a place like that, sitting on the creaky bed in his undershirt with holes in the front of it, a can of Schaefer's beer in his hand, a whore next to him, all saggy, made up like a damaged clown, like some of the old hags who were chased away from 86th Street by the cops.

There are places like that, plenty of them, but this wasn't one of them. This was a place for people with money, plenty of money, their own money, expense-account dough, money that had been stolen at the point of a gun, but anyway money and plenty of it.

"When I bought this house I got the best decorator in New York to furnish it for me," the Tiger said. "Most people like it."

He was as proud of the whore house as a man would be of his split-level house in the suburbs. He switched on the radio and turned it low to a station that was playing sweet jazz. There was a bottle of gin and some tonic and ice on a tray. He mixed a drink, not much gin, plenty of ice, and handed it to me.

"Take it easy with this, kid," he said. "I don't suppose you're used to booze. Just sit down and relax. I'll send up someone you'll like. Her name's Doreen, a nice kid from Alabama."

She was a beautiful girl, seventeen, maybe eighteen, with long glossy black hair and deep-set black eyes, a real brunette, with a touch of gold to her skin. She wore a kind of evening dress, stark white satin that shimmered like liquid in the twilit room. She had long slender thighs and small hands.

"Fix me a drink, will you, honey?" she said.

The accent was deep South. I had never heard it before except in the movies and it went through me, just the voice, as if she had run her fingernails up and down my spine. My mouth was dry and I was scared. Scared but excited. I poured out the gin, put ice in the glass and filled the glass with tonic water. My hands were shaking. She was a girl of my own age, a beautiful girl of the kind you see on pin-up calendars, and I was afraid because I didn't know what to do. I was seventeen, or almost seventeen, and alone in a room with a beautiful girl who was almost naked and I did not know how to begin. Other people knew what to do. They knew how to score anywhere, in an alley, on the roof of a tenement, in the back of a car. I didn't know how to begin. I knew that something was happening to me and that it was important but I didn't know the opening move.

I didn't have to know.

Doreen sipped her long cool drink. I finished what was left of mine. I had never tasted gin before and the warmth of the liquor spread through me, making my lips tingle.

"Just relax, honey," said Doreen. "Lay down on the bed and relax. There's no hurry. Just relax."

I lay on the big soft bed and she sat beside me. Her lips were moist and very red though there was no lipstick on them. She smelled cleanly of expensive soap. Her hair smelled fresh as if it had just been washed. It was my mother's smell, the smell of soap and a clean body, the smell of dark washed hair.

"Don't be afraid, baby," she said. "Just relax, honey child. Just take it easy."

She was an artist, a hundred-dollar whore, but she was as kind as a mother to me. Her hand moved across my body. I was on fire. Then I was naked and all at once she was naked too. She stood up, just for a second, and I heard the long zipper of her dress. It was like the sound of silk being torn. Then she was with me on the bed, her rose-colored skin smelling of the bath, her long clean hair touching my skin. She kissed my ears and my mouth and touched me with the tips of her fingers.

She was a hundred-dollar whore but she wasn't a whore at that moment. She was a woman making love. Underneath me her face was white against the black hair that was sprawled on the pillow. I kissed her on the mouth and held it there. I was in charge. I was a man. I could feel it in my blood, the sense of my manhood. I was a man and there was no one in the whole world except me and the girl who was underneath my body, around my body, this little Doreen with her bright clean hair. And then for a little while there was just me ... no one in the world but me.

I lay on the bed with my eyes closed, letting my heart run down. When I opened my eyes Doreen was smiling.

She fixed me another light drink. I lay on the bed and watched her. She took a long slug of straight gin, tossing back her head like a man in a bar, then mixed a light gin and tonic for herself. She handed me a glass, then sat down in a deep green velvet chair. The light fell on her face and breasts. She was still beautiful. And there was a kind of courtesy that was bred into her. She knew it had been my first time with a woman. She knew that a few minutes earlier I had been a scared kid, operating on a few ounces of gin. But she never let me know she knew it. She had an instinct for kindness.

I offered her money. She wouldn't take it.

"You're a guest of the house," she said.

"What about you?" I asked.

"I'll get paid," she said. "I always get paid, sugar. But if I didn't this time, I wouldn't mind."

She knew how to say the right thing, how to make you feel important. She put on her white dress, brushed out her hair, kissed me and said good-by.

There was a black tile bath that connected with the bedroom. I took a long warm shower and rubbed myself down with a big purple towel. I felt good. Standing there with the big five-dollar towel in my hand I wished that Conny Donovan could have seen me with Doreen. If he had seen Doreen, I thought, he wouldn't have very much to say about scoring with that pig Sadie Cusack in a filthy hallway with dog dirt on the floor. I had a sudden vision of Donovan squeezing his acned face in front of a splayed mirror. I swelled with contempt. He was a slob and a slob's life was the only kind he would ever know anything about. Send him to Fordham College, he would still be a slob and his life would still be a slob's life. I was different. I could feel it. I could smell it in that rich room.

I put on my shirt and pants and ran a comb through my hair. Then the Tiger knocked at the door and came into the room.

He had changed into a lightweight black silk smoking jacket, the initials L.J. embroidered on the pocket.

"How did you like Doreen?" he said.

"The most," I said. "The greatest."

"You wouldn't believe it, but six months ago she was just a scared little hustler from Alabama," he said. "Now she's got class. Real class."

He looked me over, then touched my shirt. It was a cheap T shirt, three for a dollar in the work-clothes store on Third Avenue. It was tucked into cheap chinos that had come from the same place.

"It could be the same way with you, Vincent," the Tiger said. "Put you into a good suit, get you to a decent barber, you'd look as if you went to Princeton."

I had been riding high on the gin and the sense of triumph with Doreen. Now the fear came down like a knife, sharp and anticlimactic.

"I don't know," I said awkwardly. "I can't make up my mind."

I was trying to apologize for my own lack of courage. Somehow it seemed ungrateful not to go to work for the Tiger, but there was a thread that held me back.

"Take your time," the Tiger said. "I just wanted to get acquainted." He wrote a telephone number on a card and handed it to me. "You can always call me," he said. "I'm mostly around here at night. And you don't have to make a big production out of it. I've got people working part time, whenever it suits them. I've got one girl, really good-looking, who is taking a Ph.D. up at Columbia. School teacher. Beautiful girl. She comes here on weekends when she feels like it and sometimes she takes calls at night."

I put the card into my pocket.

"Keep out of Central Park, kid," the Tiger told me. "Take my advice. Stay away from the rough stuff. There is no future in it. Only maybe a broken head."

The colored maid showed me out of the house and I passed through the lobby where the fake nurse sat, a vase of real flowers on the desk beside her. What a gag! I thought. The Waverly Nursing Home. It did not fool the police, I found out later. They were paid off, and plenty. But it took care of the neighbors and accounted for people coming and going at odd times in the day and night.

I felt the blast of the summer's heat when I went through the door of the air-cooled house, but after a few minutes I realized that the night was really cool. I walked west along the dark Village street under the neat small trees. It was dead quiet, nobody on the street but me. There was a faint breeze, just enough to make the leaves of the trees rustle, and you could feel the cool of the morning after the hot summer's night. Here and there, high up, an oblong of light showed at somebody's bedroom window. I moved through the street without making a sound on my rubber-soled sneakers.

I had the feeling you can get in New York, the feeling that I was alone in the city, as if everyone else had been killed or paralyzed by some kind of nerve gas.

I never feel it here in the madhouse. Always I am aware of the others around me, the fellowship of the afflicted, and always too I am aware of the armed guards, the line of skirmishers that protects us from those outside who would do us harm.

But in the City of New York I felt it, late at night and sometimes on an empty Sunday, the sense that I was in a deserted city, that I was autonomous, that I could cause the city and perhaps the planet to vanish simply by waving my hand.

I came through Christopher Street into Sheridan Square, almost blinded by the bright lights. There were people here and places open, a little slab of lighted world, hamburgers and hot dogs frying behind the plate-glass windows.

The sense of high autonomy vanished. I signaled to a cab going uptown. The driver just laughed at me: a punk kid in T shirt and sneakers. I cursed myself and the city. I had a pocketful of money and I couldn't get a cab.

I rode uptown on the subway—West Side—and caught the bus at 86th Street. Things were quiet up there. The gin mills were empty and the barkers outside the honky-tonks had no one to bark at. An off night. A Tuesday night. Sometimes the street was that way, looking like a tawdry traveling circus about to be disbanded. The next night it would be rolling, hundreds of people crowded together in the harsh blare of the music, jostling crowds on the wide sidewalks.

I stood on the corner for a few minutes not wanting to go upstairs. I wasn't scared. I felt no flush of dark Hebraic guilt. What I felt was simple. I did not want to go up those smelly stairs to that smelly apartment, or to look at my smelly old man stinking of sweat and beer, I wanted to keep for a little longer the fragrance of luxury that was on my flesh.

After a while I went up. There was no place else for me to go except back to the Tiger's house and I wasn't ready to do that.

I came into the apartment without making any noise. It was hot inside and the old man's door was wide open. He was on the bed in his undershirt, three empty beer cans on the floor; one arm hanging over the edge of the bed so that his fingers grazed the floor. He was naked from the waist down as usual, and the moonlight played on his body.

I stood in the doorway and looked at him. Jesus, what a pig, I thought. Suppose my aunt should get up to go to the john or something. Here was this ape, bare-assed and snoring, with his mouth wide open. No sense of shame.

I tiptoed into the old man's room and covered his body with the wrinkled top sheet which had fallen to the floor. No matter how hot you must always be covered, I thought, even if it's just with a sheet. That had been a theory of my mother's. Otherwise, she had warned us, you might catch your death in the chill of the summer's night.

CHAPTER EIGHT

WOKE up early the next morning. The old man was gone, to be on the scaffold by eight o'clock, but my Aunt Theresa was in the kitchen wearing a starched cotton dress, some kind of net over her hair. Her pocketbook was on the kitchen table beside her coffee cup. I knew exactly what was in it. A wallet with a little money and photographs of me and my mother, a prayer book and a miniature rosary in a little square plastic box with a cross on the outside. She would sit in the subway riding downtown to City Hall saying her beads underneath the copy of the *Daily News* that she bought every morning at the newsstand on the subway corner. As far as I knew her that morning, she was predictable as a cop on his beat. It was impossible to imagine that she would ever change or break out into the open.

I started to pour myself some coffee but before I could get to the stove she was on her feet.

"I'll get it for you, Vincent," she said. "And what would you like for your breakfast? Some eggs? Bacon?"

I hated breakfast in the summertime. When my mother was alive I ate it even if I choked on the eggs because she thought that breakfast was good for you, and sometimes I did the same thing for my aunt. The taste of the gin was still in my mouth that morning and the idea of eggs was enough to make my stomach heave.

"Toast," I said. "Just some toast. It's too hot to eat anything else."

"You need more than that in the morning," she said. "You're still a growing boy, Vincent. You have to eat."

"I'll throw it up," I said.

She gave me a cup of coffee and put bread into the toaster, standing beside it waiting for the bread to brown. She looked at the toaster, not at me, and said carefully, "You know, Vincent, I always promised your mother that I would look after you if anything happened to her. And I've tried to keep that promise."

"So what's wrong with me?" I said, all at once on my guard, wondering what was on her mind, wondering who had been talking to her.

"Not a thing in the world," she said. "It's just that I wish you wouldn't stay out so late."

"Did the old man tell you to speak to me?" I said. She shook her head.

"He probably doesn't even know what time I get home," I said, all at once childish and petulant.

"He works hard," my aunt said. "He needs his sleep."

"And his beer," I said.

She kissed me on the cheek. I smelled her five-and-dime cosmetics and the stuff she used on her hair.

"I know you're a good boy, Vincent," she said. "It's just that I don't like the idea of your being on the streets so late. We were talking about it at St. J———'s. Gangs and dope and everything else."

"Aunt Theresa, there aren't any gangs in this neighborhood," I said logically, and speaking the truth. "What do you think we are, a bunch of P.R.'s? Maybe in Harlem there are gangs. Maybe in Brooklyn. But not around here."

She buttered the toast, cut it into triangles and put the plate on the table before me.

"Try to get home a little earlier," she said. "I don't sleep, really, until I know you're in the house."

She sat down opposite me to finish her second cup of coffee. I looked at her, feeling a sudden flash of guilt. Suppose the cops had held us the other night, I thought. Suppose they had made the old man come across town to get me. Suppose they had told him the whole story. It wouldn't have bothered the old man. In his book clouting a pervert who had made a pass would have called for awards and decorations.

But my Aunt Theresa....

I looked at my Aunt Theresa, seeing my mother in her, almost the breath of my mother in her. To hurt my aunt would be in some way to hurt my mother. I felt guilty and protective toward her. I held her hand for a moment. It was thin and cool like my mother's hand.

"After this I will let you know where I'm going and what time I will be home," I said. "That way at least you won't think I've been hit by a car or locked up."

"Thank you, Vincent," she said. "You're a good boy."

She brushed out her hair, picked up her purse and her cheap white cotton gloves and went off to her day's work. I sat at the kitchen table drinking a second cup of coffee. The bells of St. J———'s had not yet struck nine but already the heat was gathering strength, preparing for the blasting heat of noon when the billboard thermometers in full sun would go way over a hundred degrees.

I was lonely and bored, filled with guilt and with a yearning to improve my character for the sake of my aunt who was like my mother. Vaguely I thought I would look for a job, for something to help pass the days. I swallowed the tepid coffee and shook my head, trying to shake my mind clear so that my thoughts would pass through my brain in the sequence I wanted.

A job, I thought. Any kind of job. That would be the answer. I would go downstairs and get the *Times,* look through the Boys Wanted ads.

But I am not a boy, I thought. I do not want a boy's job.

I began to sweat. My thoughts refused to be organized. I could not see the shape of any future that might be predicted for me in the classified columns of *The New York Times.* Nor could I see any future for which the Jesuits might prepare me. There was my life, looming ahead, impalpable as a rainless cloud. I would not be a man like my father, the bull. I would not be a priest like Father Murtagh. I could not see myself somehow in a college or an office or a judge's high black chair. I was lonely as a Jew in a strange land. My illness was at the core of my soul like a concealed grenade. I sat in the heat of my mother's kitchen, the steady beat of the city around me, and I had the sense that my mind was fractured.

My mind, that the priests had praised....

It was inflamed by the night before. I smelled the skin of my forearm. There was a hint of the scent that had been given off by the costly soap at the Tiger's house. I took a long lukewarm shower, then turned on the cold water, rubbing life into my skin. My memory clutched at the night before. I yearned for the murderous love of my mother.

I went downstairs, bought the *Times* and carried it to Gracie Square. I sat on a bench under an enormous sickly tree and tried to bring my eyes to focus on the long columns of small type. The Nausea swept over me. I recognized it. I was literate. I called it the French Disease. The newsprint seemed to melt in my hands, to drool in my sticky fingers. I dropped the paper to the ground. An old bum with bargaining eyes sat on the bench beside me. "Your paper?" he said cautiously.

"Take it," I said. "I'm through with it."

I wandered alone through various streets haunted by the clean smell of Doreen and by the smell of the Tiger's white car, the smell of rich new leather. In my pocket I carried the Tiger's card, paper stiff as a starched collar, the Tiger's name in raised letters: Mr. Lawrence Johnson.

I did not use the phone number that was written on the card. I was not quite ready to enter the country that is beyond good and evil. I was held by habit, by vague fear, by concern for my aunt, and by lack of motive.

Two weeks later I was seventeen and a few nights later I had my motive.

I left the house at eight o'clock. Since I had promised my aunt at breakfast I had briefed her every night.

"I'm going to the movies," I told her. "I will be home by twelve-thirty. No earlier. No later. Okay?"

I left her alone in the house with her prayer book and the TV. The old man was in Murphy's drinking beer. I saw him through the barroom window as I cut south on First Avenue. It was like a hundred other summer nights except that I went home early.

I cruised across 86th Street. All of the movie houses were running pictures that I had seen or that I didn't want to see. For some reason I didn't feel like going out of the neighborhood to a show.

The neighborhood was dead, the way a neighborhood is sometimes … just nobody around, nobody on the street corners, nobody in the candy stores. I walked as far as Gracie Square and looked at the Mayor's big frame house. There was a cop at the gate playing a game with his night stick. The park looked hot and empty. I walked back slowly toward York Avenue. What the hell, I thought, I might as well go home. It's too hot to stay on the streets.

It was nine-thirty, a time when I was never home during the summer months. I don't think I was especially quiet when I came into the apartment. I just wasn't especially noisy.

The place was dark. Even the TV set was turned off. For a moment I thought my aunt might be at St. J———'s Church for a meeting of the Catholic Young Women's Club, but it was the wrong night for that. I stood still, hardly breathing. Jesus, I thought. Maybe somebody came into the place by the fire escape window and slit her throat. I peered into the dark shadows, looking for an intruder. Then I heard him, in my aunt's room. I could hear the old man's voice: "Ah, Theresa, for the love of God. For the love of God." And then I heard my aunt's voice: "All right, Michael, I can't fight you. May the good Jesus forgive me. Mary, forgive me!"

I stood still, just inside the door. I was in shock. I could not move. I could hardly breathe. But I could hear. I could hear the springs of the bed move as I had heard them once before. I heard my aunt give a kind of gasp and cry out: "Mary, Mother of God, forgive me!"

Then I moved forward slowly on the tips of my sneakers, not making any noise. The door to my aunt's room was open and I could see them in the light from the courtyard that came through her window, secondhand defunctive light that came from the windows of other people's houses. I saw the two-backed beast on the bed; my heart was caught in my throat.

I wanted to kill them both but I could not move. For a million dollars, for my mother's life, I could not have moved from my position just outside my aunt's door. I watched them and I heard them. He was moving like a pile-driver, a big hairy piledriver.

I stood there wanting to kill them, but paralyzed. It was as if I had been on the bed with them and could not move until it was over.

Then all at once it stopped. The big piledriver stopped. It was as if the air had been let out of a big balloon. There was a long dying sigh. My aunt saw me. She tried to scream but what came from her mouth was a sound like somebody being strangled. A death-rattle kind of sound that went through me like electric shock.

It broke the paralysis. I turned and ran to the kitchen. There was a long knife on the table, a strong knife with a wide blade, the kind they call a French chef's knife, lethal as a bayonet. I grabbed it up and ran back. He was still on top of her, just beginning to move. I started toward him with the knife in the air and then my aunt really screamed. The sound curdled in the little room. He turned just as I brought the knife down hard. The point struck his shoulder and the blade went into his flesh, two inches, maybe three.

He is a bull and tough as a bull, tough as a Spanish fighting bull of the kind they had in the Hemingway movie. He hit me once on the jaw, then pulled the knife from his flesh and threw it on top of my aunt's dresser. His shoulder was bleeding pretty well but it didn't seem to bother him.

He had hit me hard enough to knock me back against the wall but he hadn't knocked me out. I grabbed the knife and made for him again. It was no use. I could never kill the bull the way the matador did it in the movie. He got hold of my arm and twisted. I did not let go of the knife. At least in my mind I did not let go, but my arm was numb and after a few seconds the knife simply slipped from my hand. Then he hit me, twice in the face and twice in the stomach, fierce short professional punches. I dropped to the floor like a bag of sand. I smelled the dust of my aunt's carpet. He stood above me, naked and hairy as an ape, the strong knife in his hand. He looked like a Roman legionary out of my Latin book. For a second I thought he was going to kill me.

Blood for blood. Then I thought: He is going to piss on me. He is going to piss in my face. I tried to get up but he pushed me back to the floor with his foot.

"You stay where you are," he said.

He put the knife on the dresser again. His shorts and under-shirt were on the floor beside my aunt's bed. He picked them up, taking his time. He wore those jockey shorts, tight-fitting in the crotch. Standing there in that light he looked like an ad for a strong-man course, taller than real life and broader than the back of a garbage truck. I wanted to kill him but I remember thinking as I lay on the floor: You might just as well have tried to kill a garbage truck.

My aunt was on the bed crying. It was a lousy sound, the sound of a sick animal dying. She was crying and crossing her-self, trying to utter her prayers through the crying.

"You whore!" I yelled. "You dirty rotten whore!"

"Shut up," said the old man. "Shut up or by all that's holy I'll kill you with my own hands."

"Go ahead. Kill me," I said. "She's still a whore. A dirty whore."

"Get up from the floor and get out of your aunt's room," he said.

His foot was back. He would have kicked me. I got up and steadied myself on the edge of the dresser. My stomach hurt where he had hit me and my hands were trembling. The words were running through my mind like peanuts dropping out of a machine: *Kill him, kill him, kill him, kill him.*

I felt his hand on my forearm. He pushed me in front of him into the parlor. "Sit down and don't move," he said.

I sat in a hard straight chair, staring at the dead metallic gray of the TV screen. He could see me from his room while he was putting on his pants. He pasted a big Band-Aid over the cut in his shoulder, then put on a clean T shirt. Then he went to the refrigerator and got himself a can of beer. I could feel his mind turning over.

"Do you want a can of Schaefer's?" he said. "I know you drink it on the outside."

"All right," I said.

I sat on the hard straight chair fighting for self-control. I felt the shock wave of the illness as I had felt it when my mother died. This time I would not surrender. I was experienced. The sickness passed over me like repetitive waves of surf, but I would not give in and submit to the morphitic peace the illness would bring me if I relaxed for an instant. It was as real as the voice of God, the illness that now washed my body. Surrender yourself, it seemed to say. Surrender your personality and all the pain will go away.

The old man came into the room, a beer can in either hand. I took the can he gave me. He sat down in his big chair that faced the television set. Behind him on the wall were his medals. From another wall the eyes of the prelates gazed upon him from their frames.

I looked up at the medals, a few cents' worth of tin and a few cents' worth of ribbon they had given to him because he had killed sixteen people. Then I looked at him. He fixed his eyes on the carpet.

"I'm sorry for what happened," he said.

"I know," I said.

I was all craft now. Play it cool, my mind said. Play it sweet and cool. Pretend the fight has gone out of you.

From the bedroom came the sound of my Aunt Theresa's weeping. My Aunt Theresa, I thought. There she sits on the dirty bed crying like a little kid, and all the time she is a dirty whore just like the other dirty whores who cruise on 86th Street looking for soldiers and sailors. My Aunt Theresa with her rosary beads in the subway and her Hail Marys all over the place. My Aunt Theresa who couldn't say shit if her mouth was full of it. My Aunt Theresa who looked like my mother, who had promised my mother....

I stop the film of my memory for a moment.

Here in the madhouse bean field, standing in the mountain sun, I remember my mood as I faced my father. I was filled with holy anger, relentless as an ancient Spanish priest. I was right and they were wrong; my mind admitted no shades of meaning but functioned with cruel clarity.

"Your aunt and me, we are going to get married," the old man said apologetically. "I should have told you, only you are a funny kid. I didn't know how you would take it."

"You married my mother," I said. "How can you marry her?"

"Vincent, your mother is dead," he said, crossing himself with the can of Schaefer's. "She has been dead going on a year. I'm only human."

I shook my head. It was a point I did not concede.

"She's dead and gone," the old man said. "As far as your aunt goes, what I did was wrong. I admit that. I ought to have waited. But I got drunk one night, so it happened, and that is that."

I said nothing. The illness had attacked me again, waves of it, striking me with force. Sitting in the chair, my back straight, my feet on the floor, I seemed to myself to stagger. I fought it back.

"You are only a kid," the old man said. "I try to talk to you man to man, but you're only a kid. In a couple of years, three years, maybe, you will understand how it is with a man."

My aunt came into the parlor. She wore a striped cotton bathrobe. Her hair was loose. Her face was blank with pain. She moved toward me with her arms out.

"Don't touch me," I said. "Don't put your hands on me."

The arms fell.

"Vincent, forgive me," she said. "Don't turn against me. Try to understand."

I sat in the hard-backed chair, rigid as a prisoner prepared for execution. My aunt retreated.

"I'm going to do the right thing," the old man said. He held the empty beer can, studying it for a moment, then squeezed it flat with one hand, a strong man's barroom trick. The effort started the wound in his shoulder. Bright fresh blood showed like a flower on the fresh white cotton of his undershirt.

"You had better go down to the dispensary and get your shoulder fixed," I said.

Con him for now, my mind told me. Don't say anything that will make him hit you again. Con him into thinking he has got you licked.

He looked at me, then looked at the blood on his underwear. Then he glanced toward my aunt's room.

"Don't worry," I told him. "I lost my head, that was all. I won't lose it again. You'd better go and get a stitch in your shoulder."

He seemed to be glad to have an excuse to get out of the house. He spoke to my aunt for a few seconds, then put on a loose sports shirt and went through the door. I listened to his heavy steps as he went down the stairs.

My aunt was there in the bedroom. I could kill her now, with the knife or with my bare hands. But I did not want to kill her then. It would not have hurt her to be killed then. She might even have welcomed the punishment. I wanted to kill them both together when he was on top of her, inside her body.

I went into her bedroom. She was sitting on the edge of her bed, her chin in her hands, staring at a point on the wall. Over the bed was a crucifix that a friend had brought her from Lourdes. I took it down and held it under her nose.

"Look at it," I said. "What's the matter, are you scared of it? It's only a hunk of wood. What are you scared of, a hunk of wood?"

She looked up at me, her blue eyes sluggish with guilt. "I am scared," she said. "I haven't been to confession for three weeks."

"Be a good Catholic," I said. "Sweep it under the frigging rug." I held the crucifix under her nose again. "I ought to shove this up you," I said. "I ought to shove it right up you."

She was off the bed and on her knees.

"Don't Vincent," she pleaded with me. "You wouldn't hurt me. I told your father you wouldn't hurt me."

"I wouldn't dirty my hands," I said.

I tossed the crucifix to the floor. She picked it up and kissed it, then crossed herself.

"Don't lose your faith, Vincent," she said. "Whatever happens, don't lose your faith in God."

"I got it right in my back pocket, close to my behind," I told her. "What I haven't got is a suitcase, so I am going to take yours."

"Where are you going?" she said.

"Away," I answered. "A long way away. As far away from you as I can get."

"You're under age. You can't go," she said.

"Do you think any judge will make me stay here if I tell him what has been going on between you and the old man?" I said. "Unfit home, that's what he would say. That's what any judge would say."

In a neighborhood like Yorkville you pick up quite a lot of information about how the courts will behave in family cases. She knew that I was right.

I was right. I was as right as the wrath of God. I had an absolute conviction that I was right and that I had been wronged. There was no mercy in me.

I took my aunt's suitcase out of the closet and carried it into my room, putting it on the bed. I didn't have a lot to pack—a few shirts and socks, underwear, a spare pair of khakis. I put in my mother's picture and then my comb and some stuff from the bathroom. Then I put on a tie and my jacket. It was the first time I had worn a tie since school let out for the summer and the collar felt tight around my neck. I was growing. I put on my jacket even though I knew it would be too hot. My school uniform hung in the closet, the shoulder patch showing up, red, white and blue: R.O.T.C.

That I will leave for him, I thought. He always liked the Army.

I closed the bag and snapped it shut. It was a blue cloth bag, a woman's bag, but I figured it didn't matter. I picked it up. On the way out I stopped at my aunt's door.

"Don't forget when he gets back to tell him what I said about the judge," I told her.

"Vincent, don't go," she begged. "I promised your mother."

"Go to hell," I said.

I went out of the apartment and down the smelly stairs. For the last time, I said to myself. For the last lousy time. Whatever happened, I promised myself, there was one thing I was sure of: I wasn't ever coming back to this Yorkville trap. Not ever in my life.

In the street I stopped for a minute, looking to the right and left. A crummy street for crummy people, the whole street rotting away behind the dirty fronts of the houses. It was a trap, this street, the trap that had caught my mother and squeezed the life from her body.

I headed west, walking for a block before I caught the bus. At Fifth Avenue I got off. I stood on the curbstone under a tree, my aunt's cheap bag in my hand. I must have known where I was going but I wanted to pretend that I had thought it out.

I sat down on a park bench, sweating because of my collar and jacket. A little way off was the art museum, floodlights playing on it, like a moving picture of Paris. The light bounced from the stone façade making viridian lace of the trees. People walked up and down on the margin of the park, not queers and Puerto Ricans the way it was on the other side of the park but ordinary people in nice clothes, just walking in the summer night. The air was heavy with the smell of the park. I took a deep breath and held it, then let the air out slowly, as if in this way I could get the air of the neighborhood out of my system.

I felt sick.

I had the sensation you get when you wake up after you have been ill with a fever and find out that the fever has broken. You feel better but you miss the fever too, and you don't quite believe it has gone. You lie there with your head on the pillow afraid to move because you don't believe you won't be dizzy and nauseous. Then after a long while you begin to emerge, as if you were coming out of a shell. That is the way I felt sitting on the bench that hot night with my aunt's bag on the bench beside me, thirty dollars in my pocket.

I sat on the bench in the darkness, thinking. The Jews have a thing they do when one of their sons goes bad or marries a Christian girl. They sit *shiva* on him. That means they declare him dead. From then on as far as they are concerned he does not exist. If they pass him on the street they walk right through him. That is what I did that night, sitting on the bench beside the park. I declared them dead, my aunt and my old man, the pair of them, dead as doornails.

I am an orphan, I said to myself. From now on I am an orphan.

"What am I waiting for?" I said to myself out loud.

I got up and flagged a cab that was bearing down Fifth Avenue. I was wearing a tie and jacket, so the cabbie took me. The son of a bitch, I thought. Or maybe it was the suitcase. I gave the driver the address of Easy Tiger's place in the Village and sat back taking it easy, smoking a cigarette as we moved downtown, away from the place where I had been born.

The Tiger was there in his red office, red leather chairs all around him, rich red curtains at his back. He looked at me, then he looked at the suitcase.

"Are the cops after you?" he said.

I shook my head.

"What's with the suitcase?" he said.

I sat down in one of the deep red chairs and told him what had happened. He was almost a stranger, a colored pimp, a man I had seen only once before, yet I talked to him in a way I could never have talked to my aunt or my old man or any priest I had ever met.

I trusted the Tiger.

That was what it came down to. I trusted the outlaw, the criminal pimp. I knew that he wouldn't try to con me. And I knew that if I told him the truth he would believe me.

He let me talk until I was all talked out. Then he poured out a glass of brandy and handed it to me. I drank it all at once and shuddered. My head was full of the rich fruity taste.

"You've had a rough night, kid," the Tiger said. "Why don't you sleep on it, and we'll talk it over in the morning?"

"I made up my mind to one thing before I came in the door," I said. "I won't go back to the neighborhood for the cops or anyone else. They will have to kill me first and take me back in a box."

"We can fix it so the cops won't find you," he said. "In a town like this one you'd be surprised how easy it is to get lost. It happens every day. Thousands of people, every year. All ages, all sexes, from all over the world. They just get lost in New York. The city swallows them up."

I nodded. I remembered people from the neighborhood who had vanished: the Riorden girl, who had been sixteen; old man Kelley, the motorman, half a dozen others vaguely recalled.

"Now you'd better get some sleep," the Tiger said. "You look like something the cat dragged in."

I stood up, swaying a little. I was beat up, so tired I could hardly stand. Then I looked at the Tiger's electric clock. It was four in the morning. I wondered where the time had gone.

"Okay," I said. "Okay."

The maid who had let me into the house showed me up the stairs to a small room on the top floor. There was a studio bed and a big deep chair and a writing table with a brass lamp. It was a nice-looking room of the kind you see in advertisements for curtains and bedspreads. It might almost have been a dormitory room. The walls were painted dark green. It is a color that makes you feel safe.

"You want anything?" the maid said. "Sammwich? Bottle of beer?"

"I'll have both," I said. "A sandwich and a bottle of beer."

It was a sliced chicken sandwich, when it came, on toast with mayonnaise and lettuce. It was the best sandwich I had ever tasted. The beer was cold and bity. There was a glass on the tray but I drank from the bottle, sitting on the deep windowsill, looking down into the dark crooked street. Soundlessly the cool, dry air poured into the room through a grill. My forehead touched the windowpane. Below me the street was empty and still. Even the leaves of the trees were still. I had the sense that I was in a high secret tower room.

It had done me good to talk to the Tiger, to pour the whole thing out. Telling him the story had let off the rest of the steam that was in me. The illness was gone that had threatened me when I sat in the straight-backed chair and looked at the old man.

I finished the sandwich and the beer, then peeled off my clothes. I took my mother's picture out of my aunt's suitcase and put the picture on the writing table. It didn't look right. I put it back into the suitcase, turned off the light and got into bed between clean sheets. I was asleep in five minutes and I slept. I didn't dream or wake up in the dark to wonder where I was or what I was doing in a strange room. I just slept like a log, and I slept right through until almost noon.

A different maid brought me breakfast and I ate it in bed from one of those trays with little folding legs. *The New York Times* was on the breakfast tray and I looked through the paper as if I expected to find the news that Vincent McCaffery had departed from Yorkville. I laughed at myself. If they go to the cops at all, I thought, they won't go for several days. They will expect me home when I'm hungry, the way most kids come home when they run away from Yorkville. Let them wait, I thought. Let them wait until they die.

I got dressed and went downstairs to see the Tiger. He was in his office wearing a red silk robe. There was a silver tray on his desk with a coffee pot and a cup. You could see that he had just gotten out of bed, but this morning he was not the psychiatric counselor. He was all business. He came right to the point, like a big shot in the movies.

"You're a smart boy, Vincent," he said. "Young and good-looking and smart. You need those things but you need me too. You know why?"

I shook my head.

"Because I've got lots of friends, most of them on the police force," he said.

He made a motion with his finger and thumb: *loot.*

"In this business," he explained, "you've got to have friends in the right places or you don't last long. This town is full of tired-out little whores and tired-out little pimps, mud kickers, pavement pounders, all the time getting pulled in, sick with booze and junk and tea, living in the jungle, the lot of them, getting eaten in the jungle. I run it like a business, like a first-class European house. It is a business. Nobody gets rolled around here. Nobody gets hurt: my people or the customers. This place is a store. We've got something to sell that people want and we sell it. If you are the boy I think you are, you can make money here. A lot of money."

He looked at me candidly, then poured coffee into his cup and drank it.

"Tell me the truth, now, kid," he said. "Are you queer yourself? Even a little bit?"

"I don't think so," I told him.

"I don't think so either," he said. "It's better. You get a kid who's really a little fag at heart, he makes attachments. He begins to have preferences. And that is bad. It should be business. All business. They should get what they pay for. No more, no less."

He got up and stretched his red silk arms, then came out from behind the desk. He walked up and down the heavy carpet, talking to me. He was smooth as a banker, sure of himself.

"For the law you are eighteen," he said. "Tomorrow morning you will have a draft card, driver's license, everything you might need." He stopped and turned. "What about a name?" he said. "The first name is common enough. But the last name we ought to change to be on the safe side."

"I don't care what the name is as long as it isn't Irish," I said, the words coming out without having been processed through my mind.

"Carter," he said. "Vincent Carter. How does that sound to you?"

"Fine," I said. "It sounds fine."

CHAPTER NINE

So I became Vincent Carter, age eighteen, place of birth Windsor, Ontario, former residence Detroit, Michigan, profession photographer's model. There were pictures of me in the files of the model agency the Tiger owned. I even had a social security card.

I was a photographer's model, too. It was the first job I did for the Tiger, before I did a single trick at the house. It was a blue movie that we made in a loft building on East 17th Street. There were five of us working as actors: Doreen, the kid from Alabama, a colored girl named Patty-Lou, a Puerto Rican kid named Rita and a long-legged professional queer named Sidney, a creep with canary-colored hair. Only Doreen and myself came from the house. The other three were people the Tiger had rounded up on the phone, people he had on call.

"Take two drinks, maybe three," the Tiger told me. "Enough so you ease up a bit but not enough so you get drunk."

The building was a ruin on the outside, but the top-floor studio wasn't bad, a big room nearly a hundred and fifty feet long with three skylights cut into the roof. The walls were covered with tan burlap, pasted to the plaster like wallpaper. There were a number of white fur rugs on the polished linoleum floor and there was a big brass bed, one of those old-fashioned beds that a whole family could sleep on. There were lights and a movie camera all set up, and an ordinary camera on a tripod beside them. One guy ran the whole works. He was director, cameraman, makeup man, everything else—a deadpan character who wore black framed glasses and a green eyeshade. At the door, on a chair with no back, sat a guy who looked like a Brooklyn hoodlum, tough and hard and wearing a gun under his thirty-dollar sports shirt.

"Let's go, let's go!" said the guy with the green eyeshade. "This ain't no Hollywood production. We got one hour, no more. Let's take 'em off and get rolling."

You might not think so, but there is a kind of plot even to a movie like that one. I was the hero and the plot developed out of a contest for my favors between the three girls and the yellow-haired queer. Everybody won and the movie ended with a kind of finale that managed to get us all in.

I was nervous at first and maybe scared, but Doreen helped me out. "Just relax, honey," she said. "This is one kind of acting where the last thing on earth you want is experience."

We were in the place perhaps forty minutes, the camera-man yelling directions at us. Then all at once the lights were cut and the camera stopped. I was on the brass bed. For a few seconds it seemed pitch dark, then my eyes adjusted to the light from the roof coming through the wireglass of the skylights. It was a nice, even light. For a moment nobody moved. We looked like people in an oil painting. Then the cameraman said, "All right, folks, that's it. Let's go."

We got dressed quickly.

"You leave here one at a time," the Brooklyn hoodlum said.

They were the only words he spoke all the time we were in the studio, but all the time, in a way, you never forgot that he was there.

"I'll meet you in the Gigolo," said Doreen. "It's a coffee shop on Macdougal Street."

She went out of the studio first, then Rita, then Patty-Lou, the colored whore. The gunman held me for three minutes, by his watch, then signaled for me to go. I came out into the dreary street filled with cut-rate vitamin stores and places that sold cheap novelties. I blinked in the bright sun. People moved along the street, passing the place where we had made the movie. Cars were parked along the curb with people sitting in them. It had been the same half an hour ago when the lights were on and the camera was turning over. In this city, I thought, when the door is closed, anything can happen inside, and outside the city goes right on, breathing in, breathing out, while all those things are transacted behind closed doors: murder and rape and bloody torture. In the streets nobody knows, nobody wants to know, nobody would care if he did know, as long as it didn't involve him. That is the city. I learned that: people walking past murder and rape and silent death, with one idea on their minds: Number One. Me, myself and I.

I rode in a cab to Macdougal Street and found Doreen's coffee shop, a small place with fancy old-fashioned lamps. The espresso machine, like a chromium idol, rose from a narrow marble counter. There were marble figures in niches. It was Doreen's hangout, the place she went when she wanted to get away from the house. She was waiting for me, sitting at a little white-topped table, guys with beards all around her romancing their beatnik girls who had lots of beads and dirty necks.

She was a beautiful girl, Doreen. She had been with a thousand men, more than a thousand, maybe twice that. In Alabama, where she came from, she took on thirty men a night, and they were not the kind of men who came to Easy Tiger's place in the Village. They were rough men, steelworkers, guys fresh from the open-hearth furnace. She took them on. She was a whore by trade, by temperament and from conviction.

But if you had seen her sitting at that white table in the beatnik coffee house, you would not have believed it. You would have taken her for an uptown kid out for an afternoon of slumming. If someone had told you that she had been the prom queen at the University of Alabama you would not have argued with him. She was smart-looking and smartly dressed. She wore a dark linen dress with a white collar and her little white gloves were on the table beside her cup of espresso. Her hair was strong and clean and brushed and her fingernails were not too long and had plain-colored polish on them. Her shoes were narrow and Italian and new.

I sat down across from her and ordered the same thing she was having: black bitter coffee that smelt strongly of lemon peel.

"Hello, actor," she said.

We both laughed. People were looking us over. In that bunch of beatniks we really stood out but we would have looked good anywhere and in any crowd of people. I was wearing a new suit that the Tiger had helped me pick out, a light-weight suit from Brooks Brothers. It was the first suit I had ever owned aside from a kid's navy-blue confirmation suit. I had owned a sports jacket, jeans and chinos, and my school uniform, period. Now I had three suits, all new, and that crummy sports jacket from Robert Hall was in the garbage where the Tiger had thrown it.

I looked good. I knew that from watching myself in the dark mirrors on the wall, and I felt good too. I felt no guilt, no sense of shame, no fear.

"What will we get for the movie bit?" I asked Doreen.

"A hundred apiece, sugar," she said.

"What does the Tiger get out of it?" I asked.

"The same as any other trick," she said. "When you get fifty, he gets fifty. When you get a hundred, he gets a hundred. And don't ever think he doesn't earn it. You're a strong young kid from a tough neighborhood and I suppose you're a street fighter, but you don't know what it is to be on the turf. I do. If the Tiger sends you to somebody's apartment he knows where he is sending you."

"So what can happen?" I asked.

"Everything can happen," she said. Her face turned black. "There are some real weirdies in this world, Vincent. Guys who like to beat people with whips or cut them with knives. Guys who like to burn people. Guys who like to kill people. There have been plenty of little hustlers beaten to death and thrown into the gutter, and plenty of your kind too."

All I could think of was my old man standing over me with the French chef's knife in his hand, the lower half of his body naked. I began to tremble, my fingertips, then my knees.

"If anybody tried to beat me like that I would kill him," I said.

She touched my hand; the trembling stopped.

"If you weren't dead first," she said. "You are lucky you made it with the Tiger. Not many people do, all the way. He likes them young and clean and smart. Sometimes they're young. Sometimes they're clean. Sometimes they're smart. All three together you don't get very often. And then there is a fourth thing. You have got to be a whore at heart, and that means either you are born that way or something happens to make you that way."

"I don't think I get what you're driving at," I said.

She frowned at her cup and saucer. She had an act, a honeysuckle-and-magnolias act, but underneath it her mind was sharp. She saw things the way I did, breaking them up into little bits, then putting them back together again.

"A whore is never in the business for the money," she said. "Oh, the money's good. I like it. But there's more to it than just money. A whore is trying to say something about the God-damned world. She is trying to spit on something because something has spit on her. I don't know. It is a way of telling the whole world and God Almighty in the bargain to go screw."

She was speaking for me and she knew it. I didn't say anything.

"I am a whore," she said. "For a hundred dollars, I would screw a gorilla. For two hundred dollars, two gorillas. It suits me. If I weren't a whore I would be dead because I couldn't stand living in Cubetown."

"Cubetown?"

"In Squaresville," she said. "I'd rather be dead."

"Anyway, you like the racket," I said.

"Sure I like it," she said. "I like to booze a little at night. I don't mind being on my back if I don't have to take on the whole Russian army. And I'm getting rich, sugar. I've got an aim in life. When I've got thirty thousand dollars in the bank, I am going to take a vacation and go around the world."

"All the way?" I said.

"All the way. By myself. And first class, sugar," she said. "Strictly first class. Top deck."

I looked at her, struck by an idea. "You are not going by yourself," I said. "I am going with you."

It was not the right thing to say. It touched something inside of Doreen that she didn't like to have disturbed.

"You son of a bitch," she said, in her soft Alabama voice.

"Why not?" I said. "You like me. I like you. Why shouldn't we go around the world together?"

"Because I'm a whore and you're a pogue boy," she said. "A piece of trade. Rough trade."

I glanced at the mirror. We looked like college people on a date.

"Who would know it?" I said. "Looking at us, who would know it? We could fool the whole boat, from the captain down."

"We would know it," she said.

Then she began to cry. People were looking at her. I gave her a fresh handkerchief. After a little she stopped crying.

"I'm sorry, Vince," she said. "You meant all right, I know that. Only don't romance me, ever, unless I ask you to. If I ask you then turn it on all the way. We'll make believe it isn't an act and we'll have a good time. But don't try to make love to me ever unless I give you the word first."

"I'm sorry," I said.

She took my hand in both of hers; her hands were cool and dry.

"It's all right," she said. "In this business you hide things. You have to hide them. We've been hurt bad, both of us. I don't know what hurt you. I don't want to know. But I know it's there. I can feel it. And I don't want you to know what hurt me. The thing is, we've both been hurt hard enough to want to fix it so that nothing can hurt us again, ever. That's why we are whores, Vincent. That's why we are in the Life."

"All the same, I'd like to get into the sack with you again," I said, trying to be offhand and breezy.

"Any time," she said. "Short time, a hundred bucks. All night, two hundred. I am a high-class whore."

Then she laughed and grabbed my hand again. The bad mood vanished like a cloud of smoke.

"You're all right, Vincent," she said. "And I know where you live. Don't be surprised sometime if you find me in your bed. But remember, it is for then, for that time, for that hour, for those few minutes. That's all there is. There isn't any more."

"Why?" I said. "Why does it have to be that way?"

"Because that's the way I live now," she said harshly. "From one minute to the next one, from one day to the next one."

We walked back to the Tiger's house. The narrow Village streets were almost empty, a few young guys on the street corners, a few old Italians playing checkers on the sidewalk, sitting on camp chairs, the board between them on their knees. It was warm but not hot, not hot enough to make you sweat unless you walked too fast. We took it easy.

Doreen wanted a peach from a pushcart. They were big peaches with lots of color, the kind you see in photographs. I bought one and handed it to her. She bit into it, swallowed, then bit again.

"You want a bite, sugar?" she said.

She offered me the bitten peach. I could see the marks of her teeth, neat as a plaster impression. It had a strange effect on my mind. I stared at the teeth marks on the fruit and it seemed to me as if the fruit were flesh, soft pink human flesh that she had bitten into. It was the Nausea, the French Disease. For an instant I felt dizzy. Then I bit into the peach, took a second bite and handed it back. She finished it and threw the pit into the clotted gutter. I stopped, staring at the peach stone. It looked like something human, some part of the human body, and not like a peach pit at all.

Doreen seemed to know what I felt without my saying anything about it. She took my arm and said, "Come on, sugar. It's only a peach stone in the gutter. You don't want that. It's garbage, sugar, nothing but garbage."

She was like that sometimes. It was almost as if she could read my mind or feel what was going on inside my head at the same time I felt it without my having said a word about what I was thinking or what it was that had attracted my attention. There was something between us from the beginning, something that ran deep and that she was often afraid of, something that she fought off the way she had fought it off in the coffee house.

We had lunch at the house. You could eat in the house or on the outside, whichever you wanted. The only rules the Tiger had were that you must let him know where you were and never to get drunk in public. Outside of that you could come and go.

The living was easy. There were three maids in the house and a colored cook who also ran the service bar in the basement. The food was good. That day we had French lamb chops, double size, and fresh green beans with plenty of butter. I had always lived like a slob ... slop for dinner at home, slop for lunch at school. Stew out of a steam kitchen. Franks and beans. Stuff like that. I wasn't used to good living, but I found that I had a gift for it and I learned fast ... about food and clothes and liquor and people.

Mostly about people.

In that house you had plenty of chances to study human nature because you saw people with all their disguises off, stripped down, naked in the flesh and naked in the mind.

I worked that afternoon, a fifty-dollar trick with Mrs. Anderson.

"She's easy, a nice woman," the Tiger told me. "She may get a little drunk but she won't ever give you any trouble. Just sweet-talk her. Honey it up. She loves that."

She was already a little drunk when she got to the house. She was a brass blonde, maybe fifty-five years old, with a fair figure as long as she was wearing her corset.

I had changed into my working clothes: skin-tight black silk pants, a white silk T shirt, ballet dancer's flat black shoes. It was an outfit that made you feel sexy just to put it on. I thought it was screwy at first, to get dressed up like that, but when the Tiger explained it, it was sensible. You can't hang around naked and you would look silly in a Brooks Brothers suit.

There was liquor on a tray in the room and I poured Mrs. Anderson a drink. She watched me move across the white rug, then she reached out and touched me. The silk fitted my body like skin and showed off my body.

"You are a doll," she said. "A living doll."

Her voice was thick from what she'd had to drink and when she leaned forward to take the glass she steadied herself on my arm, but she was all right, not sloppy, not nasty, just pretty drunk, but all right.

"Aren't I lucky," she said, watching me move around the room. "There I was at eleven o'clock this morning, sitting in that God-damned fourteen-room mausoleum on Park Avenue with nothing to do. We eat out so I don't even have to make up menus for the bastard. I was sitting there looking at high noon, and it looked lousy, when it occurred to me to have a drink."

She drank from her glass, then laughed. She had a Park Avenue accent, maybe a little bit faked.

"One thing led to another and here I am," she said. "Here I am with a living doll all to myself. An old bag like me with a living doll. A dream boat."

"You're a good-looking woman," I told her. "Better than most of this young stuff that doesn't know first base from third. I like a woman who has been around."

"You got your wish, honey," she said. "Myself, I like them young. The younger the better. By the time I'm sixty I'll probably be running after boys of thirteen."

"You got a long way to go," I said. "What are you? Forty? Forty-two?"

"Don't make me laugh," she said. "When I was forty, forty-two, you wouldn't have found me in anybody's whorehouse, saving your pardon. I could get what I wanted then. Well, to be honest, not quite what I wanted, but they still came knocking."

She sat back in her chair, a nice woman, really, the way the Tiger had said, a nice woman with a good heart just eating herself to death.

"You know what my dentist said to me?" she asked. "He said, 'Mrs. Anderson, we outlive our organs. Thanks to modern science, we outlive our organs.' Well, he was wrong about that as far as I am concerned. With me it's the other way around. It is my organ that is outliving me, my little old organ that could never get enough and never got anything at home that was worth getting."

I sat down with a weak drink in my hand.

"Walk around, will you, honey?" she said. "It gets me steamed up to see you walk around in those silk pants."

I moved around and she watched me. There were Venetian blinds at the windows, the slats opened just a little bit so that the light was stagy. In that light and after I had taken a few drinks of gin, Mrs. Anderson didn't look bad at all. I sat down on the arm of her chair and put a hand on her breast. She pulled my head down into her lap. Her mouth was greasy with lipstick. I need another drink, I thought. I have to have another drink.

After a moment she let go. I poured whisky into a shot glass. I had seen my old man throw them back straight and I tried it. The Scotch was good twelve-year-old stuff, but that straight shot hit my stomach like a fist. For a couple of seconds I thought I was going to be sick all over the clean white rug. Then my stomach turned over and finally settled down.

The warmth of the liquor spread through me. I could feel the numbness in my lips almost the way you feel novocain. I was numb and loosened up, but everything was working all right, mind and body. I went back to the big chair where Mrs. Anderson sat. In a little while, as the whisky worked, she began to look better, and after that she was just another body, simply flesh that had bought my flesh.

"Undress me, honey," she said. "It makes me feel good to have a man undress me."

She stood up. She was a little woman, a head shorter than I was. I unzipped her dress down the back. She slipped out of it and stood there in her corset. She was drunk enough so that she didn't care how silly she looked, or maybe she didn't know. I got the stockings and corset off her and then unhooked the heavy brassiere. You could see the marks on her body where the stuff had held her in, all that expensive webbing and wiring.

"Make it last," she said. "We've got all afternoon, honey, so make it last."

I slipped out of my silk suit. She lay on the bed and looked at me, fat now with her corsets off, but a nice little woman, a kind woman.

"Oh, my God," she said. "Oh my living God."

She got her money's worth. It was the booze that did it, the Scotch whisky in my brain and my blood, making things easier for me. And it was something Doreen had said: "For a hundred dollars, I would screw a gorilla. For two hundred dollars, two gorillas."

I felt that way on the whorehouse bed with this woman who was old enough to have been my grandmother. I gave her what she had paid for and she was grateful to me. And all the time I was thinking: To hell with them. To hell with the whole frigging world.

In a sense I had resigned from the world in the way Doreen and the Tiger had done. I had the idea that I could make my own world where I would be the boss, where I would control everything, even the ebb and flow of time.

When Mrs. Anderson was dressed and ready to go, she took twenty dollars from her purse and gave the money to me.

"You are a doll," she said. "A living doll."

When she had gone I offered the twenty dollars to the Tiger.

"It's yours," he said. "You keep it, unless you object to taking a tip. The house got paid, don't you worry."

CHAPTER TEN

THE Life would have been too easy if all the clients had been like Mrs. Anderson. She was a nice woman, sad and a drunk but nice, without any meanness in her.

Of course they weren't all like that. There were some who were really old, gray with age under a layer of paint, so old it made you sick to touch them unless you were full of alcohol. And there were some who were drunk and mean, who made obscene and unkind remarks. And there were some who were sick, so depressed that they frightened you, as if the sickness might be catching.

And then there was the third sex.

The idea bothered me. I wasn't sure I could go along with it all the way without wanting to hit one of them or kick him in the stomach.

It was Doreen who helped me out.

"So it's a trick like any other trick," she said. "Take a few slugs of booze first. Gin is the best. And don't let it prey on your mind. You sit down in the toilet. That's filthy too, but you don't go around thinking about it afterward. You forget about it right away as soon as you flush the john. It's the same way with this business. You can't go around all the time remembering that we are all filthy."

She was intelligent and about her profession she could be clinical as a doctor, objective as if a trick she had worked had been nothing but a case history, an experiment to be performed and written up, then neatly evaluated. Yet there was nothing cold-blooded about her; it was simply a matter of detachment and lack of shame at being what she was, because deep down and hidden from me was a greater shame that I sensed and sometimes wondered about but never, after that day in the coffee house, called into question.

More than the Tiger it was Doreen who led me into the Life, made me see it as a way of life and as a way of striking back at the world and of making the world pay cash for this.

The cash was real. I didn't earn as much as Doreen but I earned a great deal of money: two, three hundred dollars a week. Some of it I spent on clothes, most of it I put into the bank.

Shame.

Here in the madhouse, in the dark, I try to feel shame for some of the things I did in the Tiger's house. I cannot feel the shame that is ordered. Perhaps it is because when I did those things my mind and my body were blurred by alcohol. Without alcohol I could not have survived. With it the things that happened to me seemed to happen in a half-world and to be not quite real.

"One thing, don't use tea unless you have to," Doreen warned me. "When you're full of marijuana your guard is down. It's not the same as liquor. And even with these queers, people the Tiger knows, it's not a good idea ever to let down your guard."

I used nothing but booze when I was working, but sometimes we smoked the stuff, Doreen and I, up in my room in the early morning, good Chicago merchandise, first-class pot that we bought from the Tiger or from a connection at the Gigolo, Doreen's coffee shop on Macdougal Street.

We would fly. We would really fly.

Sometimes that is all we did, sit in my room and smoke pot and talk, talk, talk. Or just sit, saying nothing, getting the feeling that we were flying, that we were way out in outer space.

Other times, when a certain dreamy feeling came over her, Doreen would say, "Make love to me, sugar. Romance me. Make like it is for real. Make like we are all the way out."

And we would make the big scene.

A funny thing. I knew what I was doing and so did she. I knew what I was, I knew what she was, but sometimes it was really for real, just for those two hours in that little room of mine high up in the whorehouse at four or five o'clock in the morning. It was real. I loved her all the way. She loved me. We would say the words and do the things that people do when they are in love—way out—and the words and the things were real as long as we stayed in my little room.

Other times we were just friends, just people who liked to talk and to smoke a little pot. We always got along. Always. There was no meanness in Doreen. She had a temper. She could have killed a person if she had been pressed far enough, but there was no petty cruelty in her. I never had an unkindness from her, even at the end. Even when she turned her back there was no cruelty in her.

She taught me to understand the Life during those first few weeks I lived in the Tiger's house. That is what we called it: the Life. And it is a funny kind of life, not like the one that is lived on the outside, in Squaresville.

There is a submarine quality to life in a house like the Tiger's house. You don't think about the future or about progress, the orderly passage of time, in the same way other people do. There is no real sequence as there is, for example, in school, when you go from one grade to another with the year broken up by the summers, punctuated by the Christmas and Easter holidays.

The Life was not static. There was no sense of calm. But there was no sense of the past or future. It was always this trick, this minute, this human body, the salt taste on your tongue of this human body. In the coffee house once I heard a beatnik say to his girl: "Why do I need a watch to tell me that it is now?"

That is the way things were in the Life. The hands of the clock always pointed to the same time: now. It was the one thing that bothered me, the one thing I thought I could change and still have life be the Life.

"Don't try it, honey," Doreen said. "This is the way it has to be. You start getting ideas, you'll wind up in the Laughing Academy being manhandled by the guys in the white coats."

She was right and I was wrong.

You could not change the time scheme of the Life.

One night I drank too much by accident. When I finished work I was quite drunk. Later, in the early morning, I lay on my bed in the high room smoking a marijuana cigarette. Doreen sat in the easy chair dressed in a flannel bathrobe, looking like a boarding school girl.

The words come into my mind now, as if I played them back from a tape:

"You were right and I was wrong," I said. "It is for now, for right now, this hour, these few minutes, and that is all there is to it. The future is not anything real, that has anything to do with the past.

"It is always a dream, a phony dream, like your trip around the world. All the time you are standing still, just waiting, just rotting away underneath your clothes, everything, the whole world, people and plants and animals, even the rocks and the earth and the ocean, just standing still and dying, rotting away just as surely as a dead cat rots away in an alley.

"And there is a stink, the stink of death, just as there is a stink from that dead cat. It is all around us, the stink of the whole world dying. Some people can smell it, others can't. I thought

I started to smell it on the day my mother died on the kitchen floor, but I was wrong.

"I have always smelled it. I smelled it in the piss-shit smell of my crib. I smelled it inside of my mother, where I was before I was born, wrapped up in water and blood, living next to the waste of her body, coming out of her like waste.

"I have always smelled it, the stink of death in the whole world. It is just that for a long time I didn't know where the stink came from. I thought it came only from people and places, from my old man's undershirt, from my own dirty scapular, from the hallways in Yorkville, from Sadie the pig, from the steam kitchens of the Jesuit school.

"It comes from those things but it comes from everything else too. It comes from whisky, good whisky. It comes from perfume, expensive perfume. It comes from the private parts of people and it rises from the pulp inside their skulls. It is in the air, all the air. It came from that fresh ripe peach with your teeth marks in the fruit.

"When I smell it I need to puke.

"It fills me with the need to vomit, as if I could vomit up the whole world. It will never go away. I thought once I could make it go away or move away from it, but I found out what I should have known in the first place. The stink comes from me too, just the way it comes from everything else. I am no better than a tree or a rock or a dead cat rotting away in an alley. We are all parts of the same thing. I stink of life, which means that I stink of death.

"I stink, therefore, I am."

"Way out, man," Doreen said. "Man, you are way out."

But she had heard all the words. There were tears in her eyes. She helped me out of my obscene costume, folded the clothes and put them away in my closet. Then she helped me get into bed and pulled the soft white sheets up over my shoulders. I went off at once into a deep alcoholic sleep and woke up with a hangover.

It didn't happen very often. I used the liquor in my work and I learned what were the useful amounts of gin and whisky and champagne. I did not enjoy getting drunk. It was too close to that other sickness that began with a kind of nausea.

I was not unhappy. I felt no remorse, no guilt, only sometimes a mild nausea and sometimes a sense of bafflement, as if I had awakened in a strange room. When I thought of my aunt and the old man a cold turd of hatred formed in my chest. I did not miss them. I did not forgive them. I had declared them dead on the park bench. If they entered my mind at all it was in the way the dead intrude into the minds of the living.

War, I read once, is the continuation of diplomacy by other means. For me life in the Tiger's house was a continuation of my education by other means. I saw people of all kinds and I saw them in extreme situations. They were engaged, most of them, in a process of self-vivisection, and the dark secret places of their souls were exposed to the artificial truth that flourished in the Tiger's house.

I learned a lot in those months.

I learned a lot about people and I read a lot, paperback books that I bought, regular books that I borrowed from the library, books that the Tiger let me take from his office. He was a great reader too. For a couple of years he had been at a colored college in Alabama and he had been a captain in the Army. He knew a lot and he liked me. He talked to me as an equal. Sometimes I think I got more education in the Tiger's house than ever I got from the Jesuits.

I said there was no real sequence to the Life. That is true, but the Life had a certain pattern of its own. You got to know people who came to the place, regular customers, in the same way a storekeeper gets to know his clients. Some of them turned up more or less regularly. Mrs. Anderson, for instance, or the tough, mean young blonde who lived with a rich Lesbian and got her kicks by being mean to somebody like myself.

Then there was the man from the park who had called himself Mr. Smith. His real name was Bentley. When he returned from the West Coast he came to the house to see me.

He never mentioned the park or the police station and I never mentioned these things to him. He was easy to handle, almost too easy. He came to the house half a dozen times and said hardly a word to me. He was detached in the way rich English people in the movies are detached with their servants and children. It made me uncomfortable to be treated as if I were not really alive but only a store-window dummy or maybe a dead body that was stiil useful to him.

"He makes me feel as if I weren't human," I complained to Doreen. "He treats me as if I were a thing, like his solid-gold lighter or his handsome shoes."

"Put him down as a weirdo," she said. "If all he does is to look at you in a way you don't like, you are lucky, that's all."

"He gives me the creeps," I said.

"You'll get used to him," she said.

Then, one night, Bentley had been drinking. He ordered gin for the room, a thing he had never done before, and he took all his clothes off. He put on a robe that he kept at the house, a black raw-silk robe cut like a Japanese kimono except that the sleeves were narrower. I had been waiting for him and while I waited I had been reading a harsh, sparsely lighted novel by William Faulkner. When Bentley came into the room I put the book on the coffee table beside the gin and the glasses.

Bentley made himself a drink, half gin, then picked up the book and leafed through it.

"Well, well, what have we here?" he said. "What are you, Vincent, the whore with the mind of gold?"

I flared up. "Look here, Mr. Bentley, there's no sense in your talking that way just because you've had a few drinks," I said.

I don't know why what he had said got under my skin. Most of the time I didn't care what they said, and some of them, the mean queers, seemed to get most of their pleasure out of humiliating other people. Maybe it was because the book itself had bothered me, or perhaps it was because Bentley wasn't ordinarily mean.

He bowed to me, halk drunk, swaying a little, hands in the sleeves of his kimono. "You are quite right, Vincent, I was out of order," he said.

He sat down and looked at his drink as if he were surprised to find it in his hand. Then he drank from the glass and picked up the book, turning the pages slowly and nodding.

"I wanted to make a picture out of this and really do it all the way," he said. "You know it was done once as a film, don't you?"

"I never saw it," I said.

"It would have been long before your time," he said. "Before you were born, I should think."

He poured more gin into his glass but not more tonic water. He was quite drunk, a thing that was not a part of his pattern of life, although I did not know that, that night.

"I used to make real movies," he said. "Now I make little movies to fit the television screen."

He finished his drink. I got up and mixed him another. He was grateful. You would think I had cooked him a full-course dinner and served it on a silver plate. He looked at me sadly and said, "No. I must not. I will not. I promised myself. I promised my psychiatrist. I will not do it. I will not fall in love with you."

But he did.

At least, he became addicted to me.

I had heard about it there in the house, about men who fall in love with whores and homosexuals so gone on a young boy that they almost go out of their minds. Not psychos or drunks or swishes, but intelligent men with big incomes who are savvy in everything else, off their rockers over a prostitute or a commercial kid.

Bentley.

His name was James Carlysle Bentley and he was rich. He had always been rich. He didn't need the money he made by producing television shows because he owned seven million dollars' worth of Chicago real estate and a piece of a big store in Detroit that his grandfather had started with a peddler's wagon.

He hated his grandfather, a man he had never seen. He hated him but he couldn't get him out of his mind and he kept an oil painting of the old man in the main living room of his duplex apartment.

I said he fell in love with me because that is what he called it. I don't think it was much like what other people call love except that it was possessive.

"He wants to own me," I said to Doreen. "I can feel it when he looks at me."

She shook her head. "In this house, sugar, none of the merchandise is for sale," she said. "We are like the IBM Company. Everything is for rent only."

After the night when he came to the house drunk and found me reading the Faulkner novel, Bentley began to come more often—three, four times a week. There was no sexual contact between us. We would just sit and talk for two, three hours, about books and movies and people in the newspapers.

Most of the time he was not drinking and he never again got drunk. He would order many pots of coffee and a big silver tray of sandwiches and we would sit in the big room, the one we called Number One, with all the lights turned off except for the little light by the bed, and we would talk.

He was an excellent talker and he was smart. Very smart. He could see through people in the way you can see through a plate-glass window. I gave him my story about having been born in Windsor, Ontario, and brought up in Detroit.

"Vincent, save that for the foolish peasants," he said. "Remember, I have been in the theater for twenty years and I have an ear for the common speech. You were born in this city. Somewhere on the East Side, near the address you gave to the police. The upper East Side, I should think. Kips Bay or Yorkville."

I began to argue with him.

"Don't, Vincent. You're too intelligent," he said. "And my dear boy, actually I don't care where you were born. For all of me you might have been born at the gates of hell."

One week he came to the house every day. It was at the end of this week that the Tiger talked to me about him.

"You've got him on the hook, Vincent," the Tiger said. "A big fish. A very big fish."

"To me he's another customer," I said.

"Don't be stupid," said the Tiger harshly. "You know better than that. Why do you think he comes here, just to sit and talk with you?"

"It's his money," I said. "So I'm his companion."

"Do you know what his last companion got out of the deal?" asked the Tiger. "I'll tell you. One hundred grand. One thousand yards of green money. And for six months. Of course, he was younger than you are, a punk kid of fourteen, and if the thing had gone to the courts it would have meant time for our friend, big time, in the can or loony bin. But you are still well under age. You should wind up with as much as that dumb kid. And I won't even take half. I'll take a third."

"What do you want me to do?" I asked.

"Move in with him," the Tiger told me. "That's all you have to do."

"Move in with him?" I said. "Just like that? I don't even know his address."

"He'll ask you, Vince," said the Tiger. "Don't worry, he'll ask you. He's hooked. And these guys, when they're hooked, they're worse off than a chippie on heroin. A kid is like a mania with them. That's why you will have to watch your step. Don't try cheating on him, even with Doreen."

"I like it here in the house," I said stubbornly.

"Better than a hundred thousand dollars?" he said. "Don't be slow on the uptake, Vincent. This is a business, and you are in a position to do the business some good."

There was a tone of command in the voice and under that a threat.

"You're the boss," I said.

"I will still be the boss, even after you change your address," he said.

I took the evening off and went to a movie on 86th Street. At four in the morning I sat in my room talking with Doreen.

"I don't want to go," I said. "I like it here."

"Do you think you've got a choice, sugar?" she asked.

"No," I said. "Unless I run."

"If I had the same chance, I would take it," she said. "I would go wherever the money led me."

"Come here," I said, breaking the rule. "Come here and hold me."

She came to my bed and held me close in her arms the way my mother used to hold me when I was a little boy. Sometimes, even now, I can remember the way she felt.

"Don't be afraid, sugar," she said. "I'm here with you. Don't be afraid."

The warm arms were around me, the warm Southern voice was like a caress. After a little I slept. Sometime during the early morning Doreen went off in the pale light to her own small room in the Tiger's house.

CHAPTER ELEVEN

"Just because the psychiatrists are crazy, you must not assume that the patients are sane," Dorion says to me.

I laugh with him and remember myself.

I was not insane, I am sure of that, but in some way I had deprived myself of the range of choice. I said that the Life had a submarine quality. I myself had become unrelated to the ordinary world as a great fish in the deep sea is unrelated to the land. And I was suspended in the womb of the Life in the way the fish is suspended in water.

A week after I talked with the Tiger I changed my address and moved into James Carlysle Bentley's apartment on Gramercy Park. The building was old; he liked it that way. But he had a duplex apartment that took in the two top floors of the house: twelve rooms, six bathrooms, a big kitchen, and on the upper floor a kind of serving pantry that was really another kitchen. Bentley had a cook from Saigon who spoke and cooked in both French and Chinese, but Bentley liked sometimes to do his own cooking and that's what the second kitchen was for.

"Jean-Pierre does not like to have anyone else cook in his kitchen. He is an artist," Bentley explained to me. "So I had them put a full-sized range into the upstairs pantry."

It was a very impressive apartment.

"I thought of buying a town house when I left the Coast, but they are really a bore," Bentley told me. "So I bought this building and created this apartment out of four that were here. It was all my own conception."

I had a bedroom next to his looking down on Gramercy Park, a private square that you cannot enter unless you live on it and have a key. It is a neat little green garden with beautiful trees and bushes and there are always English nursemaids in blue serge uniforms airing the expensive kids.

"Just like London," Bentley said as we looked down at the park. "Sometime I'll take you there, Vincent, if you are good."

My bedroom had two windows and two closets and two doors, one opening on the hall, the other into a private bathroom. Downstairs there was a living room two stories high, thirty feet high at least, paneled in honey-colored wood, a fireplace at either end of the room and a lot of deep comfortable chairs. There was the portrait of the old grandfather high on the wall in a place of honor, the stern, contemptuous Yankee face looking odd, surrounded as it was by Bentley's almost matched Matisses and his three Picassos. Everything that might have interfered with the decor was built into the walls—shelves, bar, hi-fi, TV.

Next to the living room was the library. Bentley had three thousand books, most of them specially bound for him in leather or in pale green buckram that was almost as heavy as canvas. He had four encyclopedias and he had the *Oxford English Dictionary:* a thirteen-volume dictionary.

Off the library was Bentley's study, a smaller room with a big desk, black leather chairs and photographs on the walls, dozens of them, of famous people, actors, actresses, politicians. There were two policemen, deputy chief inspectors and two judges— names you would know from reading the newspapers.

I thought the pictures were phony when I first saw them. I figured that Bentley had bought the photographs and inscribed them to himself. I was wrong. They were legitimate. Almost everything about Bentley was legitimate except for himself. He had money, education, important friends. He knew the right way to do almost anything. He could have sat down at the dinner table with the Queen of England or the President of the United States and no one would have suspected that he was different from the rest of the important people.

But he was different. All the way inside he was different. It did not show on the surface, but underneath he was rotting, rotting away under his skin, because he hated himself so much that he couldn't believe that other people—all of them, the whole world—didn't hate and despise him too.

The people around him, the ones he allowed to get close to him, were bought and paid for and I understood from the start that I was bought and paid for too. To him I was his property, something he owned in the way he owned the apartment and the Ferrari and the house on the dunes at East Hampton and the other house on the desert, in Scottsdale, in Arizona.

He had to own things. That was why he had arranged for me to move out of the Tiger's house. He couldn't stand the idea of anyone else's touching me once he had decided he wanted to own me.

What kind of deal he made with the Tiger I don't know. He gave me a hundred a week to spend and another hundred to put into my bank account. It was less than I had earned at the house, but the Tiger told me not to worry.

"This is a live one, Vince," he had said. "You won't come out of it a loser, believe me."

I missed the house. At first I missed it so much I could not sleep at night. I thought of walking out of the place, just getting into the elevator, going down to the street and starting to walk, anywhere. I missed Doreen and I was bored. I had a lot of time to myself, but Bentley always wanted to know where I was going and how I spent the time.

"You are too good-looking to be wandering around this wicked city," he said. "I don't want you to get into trouble."

"Why don't you hire a guy to follow me?" I said. "It won't cost much and that way you'll be sure."

"Vincent, I don't like that," he said sharply.

"So trust me," I said.

"I don't trust anyone on this earth," he said. "Especially I don't trust myself. If I found out that you were lying to me or cheating on me I wouldn't trust myself at all."

To other people I was his nephew.

"One of my dear sister's boys," he would say.

Everyone who knew him well knew that he hadn't any sister, but everyone went along with the act, including the slab-faced elevator men who sat in the old-fashioned lobby with their big hands on their thighs. "Your uncle has just come in, sir," they'd say, coming to attention like footmen in some old-time movie. It was an old-fashioned house, Victorian, and the hall men, acting like old personal servants, were all part of the gag along with the real oil paintings and the Persian rug on the lobby floor that Jean-Pierre, the cook, told me had cost fifteen thousand dollars.

Bentley's kitchen, the big one, looked old-fashioned too. There were copper pots on the walls, antique spice jars, stuff like that, but that was all on the surface. It was what Bentley called garniture. Everything that mattered was modern, the stove, the refrigerator, the sink and the dishwashing machine.

"That stove cost fourteen hundred dollars," Jean-Pierre told me. "Look: coal fire here, gas fire here, coal oven, gas oven, electric oven. Made to my order."

He had a weird accent, mixed French and Chinese, and there was a mean streak in him that made you uncomfortable. He looked at me, then touched my chin.

"You think you are the Number One boy here?" he said. "You are wrong, my little cadet. You are Number Two. Jean-Pierre is Number One. The boss, he thinks of his stomach first and of those other matters second."

He tried to grope me, fooling around. I didn't like to have him touch me. I backed away.

"You Chinese bastard," I said. "You touch me again like that and I'll brain you with your own cleaver."

There was a butcher's block in the kitchen with six cleavers hanging from a rack above it, running from big to little. Jean-Pierre grabbed the big one.

"Take one for yourself," he said. "We will see which of the skulls is split."

"You know what you can do with it," I said.

Still, I backed out of the kitchen, not taking any chances. He could split a hair with one of those cleavers. He kept them sharp as razors and used them where another cook would have used a knife. He could take a loin of pork, four pounds, maybe five. In a few minutes the meat was trimmed and cut into small even pieces, all with the cleaver.

"Oh, he is wicked, is my Jean-Pierre," Bentley said to me. "He is a very wicked boy. In Saigon, I am told, he did some very dreadful things. But I wouldn't be without him. He is one of the greatest cooks in the world."

Food was a big thing with Bentley. Food and clothes. He spent at least an hour every day in the kitchen with Jean-Pierre planning menus, reading recipes, looking over the stuff that was delivered by the private markets he used. He loved his food but he wasn't a hog. He took small portions and watched his weight, but everything that came to the table was perfect.

He was the same way about his clothes. He kept thirty suits in his dressing-room closet behind sliding mahogany doors.

"Every year I clean them out," he explained. "The lot. I hate old clothes. Twelve months. That's the limit for a suit. Then off they go to the horrid poor. I'm not one of your rich men who likes to go about with his ass out."

He had a colored valet who did nothing but take care of the clothes and bring Bentley his breakfast in bed. His name was Daniel, an ex-fighter, middleweight, who had lost an eye in the ring. Over the empty socket he wore a black sateen patch, the color just a shade darker than his skin.

There were two Irish maids in the house and a colored porter who came in on certain days to polish the floors and the brass. Five people altogether to take care of one man, or two now that I was there. Daniel lived in a basement room and the two maids lived at home, but Jean-Pierre had a little suite off the kitchen, a bedroom, sitting room and bath that many a family of three would have been glad to get.

After a while I got used to the way things went at Bentley's place. He was a man who did almost literally as he pleased. We stayed up late and we slept through the mornings, all day once in a while.

Physically there was not much between us.

"I really hate it," he said one night when he had gone through his regular dead-pan performance. "I really detest it."

"Why do you do it, then?" I asked.

"I can't help myself," he said. "And every time, beforehand, I am sure that it will be different."

"What about women?" I said. "Haven't you ever tried it with women?"

He got up from the bed and crossed the room and sat in a big arm chair. On his dressing table was a candelabrum with eight candles burning in it. He liked candlelight, especially when he wanted to feel romantic. The soft light fell on his face, flickering a little. The face was the face of a rotting statue. The eyes showed pain and fear.

"You know I like women," he said. "I like to have them around me. But I haven't tried to sleep with a woman for more than twenty years. The last time was enough, thank you."

He stopped talking for a moment and took one of his custom-made cigarettes from a silver box on the table beside him. He held the lighter open for a long time, looking at the dancing yellow flame which opposed the softer light of the candles. Then he snapped the lighter shut, making the sound a punctuation in his thoughts.

"I was a student at Harvard. She was a Wellesley girl, small and trim and blonde. She was very aggressive. I was no good. She laughed at me. I went into the hotel bathroom and was sick. All the time I was being sick I could hear the sound of her laughter. Even when she had stopped laughing and put on her clothes and gone out of the hotel by herself I could still hear the sound of her laughter."

He touched himself, then examined himself in the candlelight as if the thing attached to his body were some kind of biological specimen.

"Look," he said. "Look here. I tried to cut it off once with a straight razor. Twelve stitches the doctors took. Twelve of them, with no anesthetic. I fainted, but not quite all the way. The pain was ghastly."

I hadn't moved from the bed.

"Come and look," Bentley insisted. "I want you to see."

You could see the scar and the marks of the stitches. He had been telling the truth. I backed away from him, feeling a little sick at my stomach.

"I know," he said. "Sick, sick, sick. That's what the doctors said and I believed them. I believed them enough so that I let them put me into a hospital in Kansas for almost a year. Can you imagine me in Kansas, my dear boy? It simply made me worse."

He was no fool, Bentley. He was a well-educated man, with a degree from Harvard and a second degree from Oxford. If he had not been rich and queer in the way he was, I think he would have made a first-class college professor. I never really liked him. I was too conscious of being his property. But there were times when I respected him. I learned a lot from him, things I would never have had the chance to learn anywhere else, about food and clothes and people and books.

"You are intelligent, Vincent," he said. "Almost too intelligent. But you are vastly ignorant. You are monstrously ignorant. We must change that. You must read, two or three hours a day at least."

That was one of the moods he had, when he would treat me as a protégé, almost as a son. He was very serious about it. He drew up lists of books and asked me to write short reports on what I had read.

I read the books he asked me to read and I wrote the reports. I listened to Bentley. I studied him. I watched him. Sometimes in front of the mirror in my bedroom I would impersonate Bentley, imitating his gestures, his tone of voice, the way he used his long-fingered hands. I watched him with other people, admiring the way he handled them, the graceful way in which he served as host.

He had his purely cruel side.

"*Crime et Châtiment*," he said one day, glancing at the shelves in the library. "I don't suppose your French is adequate. Too bad. The French translation is better than the English. But the English will have to do."

He offered me a hand-bound copy of *Crime and Punishment*. I took it, running my fingers over the smooth-grained leather, looking at the gilt-stamped spine.

"Read it carefully," Bentley said. "You will have the privilege of catching a glimpse of your own imperfect soul, my boy. I see you that way sometimes. You are the poor man's Raskolnikov, watered down for the modern market. Still, in your Celtic way I suppose you're an honest nihilist, Vincent. You simply don't have the equipment to be a first-rate Russian hero."

I began the book, following the tortured Raskolnikov through the opening pages, watching Raskolnikov gather his courage and prepare himself for the murder. I sat in the library with the book on my lap, scalded by terror. I could read no further. The Russian guilt took me by the throat. I had the sensation of being strangled.

"You will read it!" Bentley insisted.

"No."

"You will read it," he said. "Every word. Or I will read it aloud to you. I swear it, Vincent. If it is necessary I will ask Jean-Pierre to tie you into a chair and I will read that book to you, word by word."

I read the novel, all of it, every word, and the experience was a nightmare that became a part of my past, present and future, an area wedged into my mind, permanent as the fact of my own birth. The ghost of Raskolnikov haunted me, causing me to wake up in the dark night.

Bentley was amused.

"You see, my dear boy, it is possible to take up evil as a profession, but one must first be certain that he has killed the last sparks of his conscience. Otherwise...."

He threw his hands into the air, then returned to the script of a play he was reading, ignoring me for the rest of the evening.

That fall Bentley was looking for a play that he could produce on Broadway.

"I'm fed up with television and Hollywood is impossible these days," he said. "Besides, the legitimate theater has always been my first love. If you will pardon the cliché."

He was reading manuscripts and talking to authors and actors. He had an office in Radio City with a secretary and a phone girl, but he went there only once or twice a week. Most of the time he used his study as an office. Sitting in the library I could hear him talking to playwrights and actors and agents—people from the William Morris office, M.C.A., all the big outfits. He knew his business. You could feel that when you listened to him talking to these professional people, and you could see that they had respect for him as far as the theater was concerned.

Once a week, sometimes twice a week, he would throw a party. He liked to give parties and he always did it in a big way. He brought in a bartender and a couple of waiters. If there were more than thirty people Daniel, the one-eyed valet, would help out, passing drinks and things to eat.

Sometimes the parties were straight. I mean that the guests would be both men and women. And at those parties I saw people in Bentley's house who were absolutely at the top of the list: movie people, stage people, politicians, college professors. One night there was a judge. Not a magistrate but a real judge from the Court of Special Sessions.

On other nights the parties were different. They were attended by people Bentley called the hoi phalloi. Half of the guests would be dressed in women's clothes, wearing lipstick, mascara and falsies—drag, they called it—and sometimes these parties got pretty rough.

Nobody bothered me. Most of the queers were freeloaders who didn't want to get on the wrong side of Bentley. I fooled around with them and danced with the ones in drag. Sometimes the way they were fixed up with wigs and pads and fake breasts you would have sworn that you were dancing with a woman. There were the really effeminate ones, and the others who got a kick out of being in drag but who liked to boom forth in a big bass voice.

Then there was the movie actor who liked to be whipped. He was a second-line star, well-known, and a he-man on the screen. One night at a big drag party I saw the whole thing happen. It was almost like a play.

The actor was wearing a white satin evening gown, low cut, with falsies that stuck out, and he had on a wig of glossy black hair. He had pancake make-up on his face and arms and shoulders. From a few feet away you would not have believed that he was not a beautiful woman.

He began to needle Bentley a couple of hours after the party started, pinching Bentley's ear, stepping on his toes, childish stuff like that. Bentley went along with the act, slapping the cowboy on the behind or tapping him on the wrist.

"You are a naughty, naughty girl," Bentley said. "If you don't behave you will have to be punished."

"Oh, you beast, you wouldn't dare," the cowboy said.

"Darling, you know I would," said Bentley.

The cowboy picked up a martini cocktail and threw it into Bentley's face. Everybody stopped talking. Bentley wiped his face with a napkin, then stood up with his fist in the air.

"You are a filthy, vicious girl," he said. "You must be punished at once."

He went to a closet in the hallway. When he came back he carried a whip, a long thick leather whip that looked like a long black snake.

"Pull up your skirts and bend over, you vicious little bitch," said Bentley.

I thought it was a gag. Then I heard the whip whistle in the air. It was the kind of sound you can almost feel as well as hear. The whip raised a red welt, then another, and then little drops of blood rose along the edges of the welts.

Everyone was watching. There was no sound in the room except for the rise and fall of the whip. Every time the whip came down the cowboy uttered a kind of moan. It was difficult to make out whether the sound was supposed to express pleasure or pain.

The hired bartender stood behind his portable bar, deadpan, polishing glasses. The atmosphere in the room was heavy as if no one was quite breathing.

This is not for me, I thought. This is not for me.

Then I got sick at my stomach. I turned away and blundered toward the guest bathroom. Someone was holding me while I was sick. It was the Chinese cook, Jean-Pierre.

"Jesus," I said. "Holy Jesus."

"Don't be silly, St. Vincent," said Jean-Pierre. "He loves it. It is meat and drink to him."

"He must be crazy," I said.

"You have a faulty education," said the cook. "It is a thing we all share in one way or another. You yourself, Irishman. You must want to be punished for something or you would not be living in this house."

I pulled away from Jean-Pierre and went back into the living room. The cowboy was on the floor. His white dress was bloodied. Bentley was wiping the whip with a clean linen napkin.

"The guy passed out," I said.

"Fainted," said Jean-Pierre, who had followed me into the room. "He always faints. That is part of the fun."

"You mean he's faking?" I said.

"Oh, he is quite unconscious, I'm sure," said the cook. "Come on, young one, let us carry him into the bathroom and clean him up a little."

I felt a mixture of pity and disgust. I helped Jean-Pierre carry the cowboy into the guest john. He was conscious now and moaning. Jean-Pierre propped him over the sink so that his backside was in the air. He washed the welts with hot water, then took a bottle of iodine from the medicine cabinet. When the iodine touched his wounds the cowboy shrieked with pain.

"You know you love it," said the cook. "*Sois sage.* Be still so I can do the rest."

I went back into the big room. The lights had all been turned off and the candles were lit. All around the room guests sat on the floor in twos and threes, giggling and squealing in the half-dark like parochial school girls on a picnic. I went to the bar and asked for gin.

"Straight gin?" the bartender said.

"Straight and a double," I said.

I stood beside the bar and drank four ounces of straight gin. I had learned to control the heave of my stomach against straight liquor and to hold it down until the muscles tightened, then relaxed. It is a trick and it worked. The alcohol flooded through my system and the drink brought tears to my eyes. Then I began to feel better. I turned away from the bar. On a table was a box of reefers, marijuana cigarettes. I lit one and sat on the floor, drawing in deeply, holding the smoke in my lungs.

After a while I began to float. All around me people were doing things that are supposed to be disgusting, but once the pot set in and I was floating six inches off the floor it all seemed wonderfully funny. I thought of the bleeding backside and laughed. This is the life, I thought. This is the only frigging life.

I was floating. I was flying. All around me thirty people were making thirty kinds of love. I was in it and not in it. I touched the tip of my nose. It was like an electric shock without the feeling of pain. I was fearless. I felt like a king, an Irish king. I didn't need anybody else for anything. I was the world, the whole God-damned world, and the pederasts in the candlelight, they were there to amuse me, if they were really there at all and not just figures in my mind put there by the gin and the reefers.

When all of the guests were finally gone I sat in Bentley's bedroom. It was almost dawn and through the big squarish windows came the beginnings of the pale morning light. Bentley was haggard and nervous; sometimes he got fed up with his parties.

"Are you tired, Vincent?" he asked.

I shook my head. "I feel groggy and beat up but I'm not tired," I told him. "At least, I'm not sleepy."

"I will order the car," said Bentley. "We can drive out to East Hampton and I will cook some breakfast for us. Then if the sun is warm enough we can sit on the deck and look at the ocean."

He drove fast, holding the low-slung Ferrari beautifully to the road. We barreled over the parkway at eighty and ninety miles an hour. All the way from LaGuardia Field to the turn-off for East Hampton we weren't below seventy and we didn't see a motorcycle cop all the way out. It was exciting, as if the highway had been made for our convenience and for this one journey, as if the road rolled up behind us after we had used it.

When the sun got a little higher Bentley lowered the windows and I smelled the air of the farmland as we passed the open fields.

"Sometimes I have to get out of the city," Bentley said. "I couldn't really live anywhere else except perhaps Paris or London, but sometimes I have to run away from New York, like this."

I understood what he meant. Sometimes when I was living in Yorkville I would get on the subway and ride all the way out to Coney Island in the wintertime just to get away from the smell of the city and the big ticking clock of the city that worked its way into your brain like a big mechanical heart. I would stand on the empty boardwalk, shivering with the fierce cold that came in from the sea, my teeth chattering, my face wet with the cold salt, and pretty soon I would turn away but I would be glad I had gone there just to breathe in the air of the ocean and breathe out the air of the city.

Bentley's beach house was empty. During the summer months he kept a colored servant there all the time so that he could arrive whenever he felt like it with half a dozen guests if he wanted to and find everything ready, but this was October and most of the dune houses were closed, some of them boarded up against intruders and the sea.

There were bright starched flags flying from the white masts at the Coast Guard station. The ocean looked like molded lead, the gray waves glittering somberly in the high morning sun. The long white beach was deserted. Out on the ocean a mile or so was a ship, a freighter, moving so slowly it seemed to be standing still, over it a smudge of black oily smoke.

We had been on the road for only an hour and twenty minutes but we were in another world. Bentley's place was on a high sand dune, built on piles driven into the sand, a low slant-roofed house with redwood sides and a glass front and a big covered deck that faced the sea. It was simple, really only a large shed with a glass front, but you could tell that it was expensive.

Bentley was proud of the house.

"You will never get a better view of the ocean than you get from this deck," he said, shading his eyes and looking out to sea. "It is a pure sea view. There is nothing like it in Europe. Only, perhaps, in the South Seas."

Bentley made coffee, then fried the bacon and eggs he had brought with him in the car. The smell of the bacon combined with the smell of the coffee drifted from the kitchen through the rest of the house. I was struck by a sense of the past, sitting in a deep canvas chair, staring at the ocean through the thermopane glass. The breakfast smell took me back in time to the old man's apartment, with my Aunt Theresa cooking bacon and eggs in that crummy kitchen where a million cockroaches lived under the soggy linoleum so that if you came into the kitchen in the dark and switched on the light fast you saw them scuttling back into dark places behind the sink and under the stove. The kitchens were different but the breakfast smell was the same; bacon and eggs and coffee and then finally the smell of toast, all blended together and taking me back in my mind to the old man's place in Yorkville.

For a few seconds I was homesick. I felt pure nostalgia. It was the breakfast smell and the ocean and the long tragic beach stretching for miles in both directions, beach and dunes and beach grass that had been planted on the dunes in rigid military formation.

I felt so homesick I wanted to cry. I was sick for the smells of Yorkville, for the familiar accents, for the bright false jewels of the neon lights.

Then the hate came to my rescue. It is a powerful ally. Pictures passed through my mind like a movie film gone crazy:

my mother dead on the kitchen floor; the old man kicking me; my aunt, dressed in stiff black, coming to the hospital to visit me straight from my mother's funeral; the two of them on my aunt's narrow bed, the old man's body working like a pump; the old man standing above me with the French chef's knife in his fist, his tough enormous manhood almost in my face; the conviction, He will piss on me! he is going to piss in my face!

It was all in my mouth, acid as death, and then there was the taste of blood in my mouth as if the sides of my face had opened on the inside, spilling blood into my throat. I sat up straight in the canvas chair and looked at the gray dangerous ocean.

To hell with them, I said in my mind. I hope they both rot in hell.

It was no good. I did not believe in heaven or hell and I knew they were not rotting or burning. I knew where they were. They were in my mother's bed, glued together like a pair of dogs in the street, or sound asleep on my mother's pillow: gross satiated innocent lambs.

"Breakfast!" Bentley called. "Come and get it, Vincent."

I shook myself the way a dog shakes off water, trying to shake the pictures out of my mind. Then I got up and went to the table Bentley had set near the window facing the sea. I looked at the breakfast on my plate. The smell was the same but the bacon and eggs and toast were different. Whatever Bentley cooked was perfect. Each egg, each piece of bacon, each triangle of toast was perfect.

I ate three eggs and seven strips of bacon. Then I lit a cigarette and sat back in my chair to enjoy the coffee. It was a special kind of coffee, grown in Hawaii, and it tasted almost like hot rich wine.

Bentley was happy. He was always happy when he had cooked a meal and served it. He looked at me across the table.

"Are you happy, Vincent?" he asked. "No regrets?"

"Sure I'm happy," I said. "As happy as I've ever been, I guess."

I wasn't happy. I had never been happy since the day my mother died and now something was gnawing at me, trying to inform me that I hadn't been happy when she was alive but only hypnotized by her love. I looked at the sea horizon. Other mothers manage to die, I thought, without murdering their sons. Why had my mother murdered me and taken the best of me with her into the raw grave in the Bronx?

I shook it off then stood up and stretched my arms.

"I'll wash these dishes," I said.

"No, I'll do them," Bentley said. "You sit and watch the ocean. It is good for your soul."

He was that way when the domestic streak came out in him. He liked to do the whole thing himself. When he was in that mood he was simple, almost in the way my aunt had seemed to me to be simple.

We drove back to the city, moving steadily through the light traffic. Other drivers stared at the car in the way they always did, with a mixture of contempt and jealousy. They were jealous because they knew that the car had cost fifteen thousand plus, but they were contemptuous of it because it was in some way effete even though it was more powerful and faster than anything else on the road. People are jealous of men like Bentley but by instinct they would not trade places with him.

I would not have changed places with him. I felt superior to him in spite of his wealth and his education and the *savoir-faire* that sometimes I imitated in front of a mirror.

Sitting beside Bentley in the cockpit of the Ferrari, which slumbered at forty miles an hour, I was struck by a helpful image. For myself, I thought, Bentley was a kind of disease, an illness that I had somehow caught or perhaps a continuation of that other illness that had knocked me down when my mother died. Or perhaps it was an illness that began at birth, that was somehow involved with my mother's love, that was more a love for the Church of Rome than ever a love for me.

For an illness there will be a cure, the orderly process of my mind informed me. As we moved into the city traffic I felt a sudden flash of hope, and instantly after this an itch, a yearning to take a decision, any decision, even the decision to throw myself out of my bedroom window.

CHAPTER TWELVE

BENTLEY had made a mistake from his point of view when he took me to East Hampton. Those few hours on the sand dunes had sharpened my sense of loneliness and highlighted my lack of purpose. There is something about the sea and the sand, the long stretches of empty beach, that touches the metaphysical impulse. I wanted to add things up and found that I had forgotten how to count. I was lonely and restless and I had the conviction that I had lost track of time. The days simply fell away like dead leaves. Time was passing, but I had no illusion that I moved with it. I was young, I wanted to shout. I wanted to spend my time, the time of my life, like money drawn from the bank, but as Bentley lived there was no time except day and night, and sometimes even this division disappeared when one of his parties ran on until nine or ten o'clock in the morning.

I had a hundred-dollar watch that Bentley had given me as a present. I didn't need it. The time of day was whatever Bentley wanted it to be.

On the surface I was having a good time. We went to the shows, on Broadway and off, and most of the time we went backstage. Bentley knew almost everyone who was connected with the theater. After the show we would go to Sardi's or to some night club. At first I had an odd class resentment. In the neighborhood gin mills, unless you are practically middle-aged, they will ask you for a draft card or a driver's license. In the fancy spots to which Bentley went I had to show my phony papers only once and then the manager came to the table to make a personal apology.

I found out that I could drink champagne cocktails and a lot of them if I didn't drink them too fast, so that is what I ordered when Bentley wanted to go out on the town. In the apartment I drank what I pleased, gin if I needed something to help black out the physical fact of Bentley. I kept a bottle in my bedroom for times like that.

There wasn't very much of that.

Most of the time what Bentley wanted from me was for me simply to be there, to listen, to be looked at, to be owned, sometimes to be baited in a clever homosexual way.

I wasn't a prisoner in the apartment. I could come and go more or less as I pleased and I always had money in my pocket. The thing was, where could I go? I couldn't go to the Tiger's house, because I knew that neither Bentley nor the Tiger would stand for that. I couldn't go to the neighborhood to show off my new clothes and my money.

So I went to the movies when I felt like it and sometimes when I didn't feel like it, because the dark womb of the movie house offered a certain comfort even when the picture was a bore. I took a series of driving lessons. I looked through the catalogues of universities with the idea that I might take a course.

"Your animal spirits are goading you," Bentley said. "I am inadequate. Perhaps you should join a gymnasium, Vincent. Exercise and cold baths. There's the remedy, my dear boy. Reilly's. A place like that."

He had chosen a play out of the two or three hundred he had looked at during the months I had been with him. Before he decided, he had two actors and an actress read the script in the living room. They must have gone through some of the scenes ten times before he had heard enough. It was one of those sick-sick plays, people in the swamps of Louisiana living in a falling-down mansion, the brother and sister sleeping together because nobody else was good enough for them. They were a creepy family, hardly ever going out of the mansion, waited on by colored people who never got paid. In the end the brother killed his sister with his great-grandfather's Civil War sword, then killed himself with rat poison mixed with bourbon whisky and water from the spring that the family had used for two hundred years.

"What do you think of it, Vincent?" Bentley asked when the hired actors had gone.

"It reminds me of Yorkville," I said.

"Don't try to be amusing, Vincent," he said. "It will cost me a hundred and fifty thousand dollars to put this play on if I do it. For your information, these days that kind of money is significant even to a Texas oil millionaire, which I am not."

"I wasn't kidding," I told him. "There are people like that in Yorkville, sixty blocks from here. Only it's not a Civil War sword. It's a shillelagh or a bit of ribbon from the Irish Revolution. Talk about living in the past. Why, my old man—"

I cut myself off. Bentley was curious.

"Yes? What about him?" he said.

"Nothing. It's none of your business," I said.

"Oh, Vincent, you're not being fair," he said. "You know I tell you everything about myself."

"Shut up!" I told him. "Shut up!"

There had not been many times when I had talked to Bentley in that way. You would think I had hit him in the face. He went into his bedroom and closed the door. I could hear him in there crying like a baby, sobbing because I had told him to shut up. I sat in my own bedroom listening to him cry. It gave me the sensation of power to be able to make him cry.

When he came out of the bedroom his crying jag was over. He looked at me with some contempt.

"I have decided to do the Louisiana play," he said. "If you don't like it, it must have merit, for you have the taste of a guttersnipe."

"It's your money," I told him, not rising to the insult.

"I should advise you not to forget that," he said.

I never really forgot that, because Bentley never permitted me to forget it, nor did anyone else in the house. Jean-Pierre, the cook, Daniel, the valet, even the two Irish maids, they never permitted me to forget it.

One morning when Bentley had gone uptown to the William Morris office I sat in the library trying to read. One of the maids was dusting the books. That was something in itself. She would never have gone on dusting if Bentley had sat down in the library. It was her way of saying that I didn't matter.

I was stubborn. I sat in my chair and would not leave. The maid was stubborn too. She went right on with her work. It was Norah, the second maid, a good-looking black-haired Irishwoman of twenty-eight or thirty. She was dressed in a nylon uniform, black and very sheer, so that I could see through it when she climbed the ladder to dust the books and her body was placed between me and the light that came through the library window. Under the nylon there was nothing but her bare Irish skin. Her stockings were rolled and tucked into a knot so that they stayed up without garters. When she reached for the higher books I could see the top roll of her stockings and the bare flesh above it, and when she was in front of the light I could see the outline of her body. It was like looking at a naked woman through a very thin black curtain.

Norah was no Miss Rheingold but she stirred me up. For weeks now I had been restless. Since the day on the beach I had known what it was. I wanted a woman. Any woman.

When Norah started to climb down from the ladder I got out of my chair and pretended to help her. I touched her body for a second, then put an arm around her waist. She backed away and looked at me as if I had been filth.

"Keep your hands to yourself," she said. "Do you think I don't know what you are, you dirty little homosexual?"

"Is that what you call Bentley?" I said. I mimicked her Irish accent. "With him it's always 'Yes, your honor,' and 'No, your honor.'"

"He pays my wages," said Norah.

"He pays mine too and I make a lot more than you do," I said, losing my temper.

"I'm not a dirty whore," she said.

"Lucky for you," I said. "Who would want to pay good money to stick it into a skivvie?"

It was the Irish word that hurt, a word I had learned from the old man. Skivvie. A word of contempt. Norah hit me with her open hand hard enough to make my eyes water.

"Would you be wanting me to tell the boss that you put a hand on me?" she said. "He wouldn't find that to his taste, you know. He wouldn't like the idea of his little pet makin' a pass at any kind of a girl at all, even a common skivvie."

"Ah, you can go to hell," I said.

I went into my room and threw myself on the bed. I rolled over and lay on my back, hands on the pillow under my head. I stared at the shadows thrown by the Venetian blinds onto the chalk-white ceiling. They were like the shadows of prison bars, running in the wrong direction.

Little, she had called me.

A dirty little homosexual.

Mr. Bentley's little pet.

I was five feet eleven and I weighed a hundred and fifty-five pounds. I wasn't little. I was good-sized. Still, automatically, she had used the word. It was that word that hurt, in the same way the word skivvie had hurt her.

I got up from the bed, took a twenty-dollar bill from my wallet and went back to the library. Norah was there, on her knees, doing the books on the lower shelves.

"I didn't mean anything," I told her. "I just get lonesome sometimes. You know. Fed up."

She looked up at me, dust rag in her hand. I offered her the twenty dollars. She took it and tucked it into the bosom of her uniform.

"It's all right," she said.

I was sorry she had taken the money. I stood there beside her, wishing that she had hit me again and flailed me with black Gaelic curses. I hated the money, the filthy money, that was clean and crisp in the hand and that curdled the sense of honor.

"We shouldn't be fighting," I said awkwardly. "I'm Irish myself."

"You're not!" she said. "What county, then?"

"Irish-American," I said. "My mother came from Clare."

She stood up, facing me, and brushed a strand of hair away from her eyes. Her pale honest eyes were on me.

"You're only a lad," she said in a half-whisper. "You ought to get out of this altogether."

"My mother meant me for a priest," I said, the words coming out of my mouth without my having thought them at all.

Norah crossed herself quickly.

"Don't be sayin' things like that," she said. "Not in this house."

"It was my mother's idea," I said.

"You ought to go back to your mother," she said. "A lad like you, fine and handsome. An Irish Catholic boy. It's a sin and a shame what you're doin'."

"Back to my mother," I said. I had a vision of the grave in the Bronx, the scurf-touched grass, the earth mound summer-parched, dry as chalk. "Maybe you're right," I said. "Maybe you're right."

After that Norah and I were friendly. From time to time I gave her money, five dollars or ten. She never excited me again in the way she had done when I saw her high up on the library ladder. After that she was just a maid, a skivvie with red knees and knuckles smelling of soap and furniture polish and religion, but she was a kind of friend in the house in the way that the cook, Jean-Pierre, was an enemy, and the valet, Daniel, a neutral.

CHAPTER THIRTEEN

I N February Bentley began to cast his play and in March it went into rehearsal, not in a regular theater but in a made-over dance hall near Cooper Union. He was trying to line up a Broadway theater.

He was out of the house a lot. Sometimes he left at ten in the morning and he would be gone all day. When he came home he was tired. I went to rehearsals for a while and then I got bored with that.

I was fed up and ever since the encounter with Norah I had been thinking about Doreen. It nagged at me, the need to see her, not just to make love to her but to sit with her and talk the way we had done at the Tiger's house when she came upstairs to my room in the mornings.

I had a pocketful of money and lots of time but there was only one thing I wanted to do and that was to see Doreen. I couldn't go to the house or call; the Tiger would know if I did that. I was even afraid to write her a letter for fear the Tiger would see it.

Then I thought of the coffee house on Macdougal Street. I began to go there every day, sitting with the beatniks and the uptown bagel babies and the middle-aged tourists who were trying to be shocked. I sat in the Gigolo by the hour waiting for Doreen to show. I must have drunk a hundred cups of espresso, sitting around, waiting for her.

Then one day at about twelve-thirty I came out of the Gigolo into Macdougal Street and there she was, all by herself, swinging along with her head in the air, all that beautiful black hair loose on her back and brushed so that it gleamed like a polished piano. It was a bright March day and warm. She was dressed in a green tweed suit, a soft green that suited her skin, and a white silk shirt open at the throat. She didn't see me. I caught her arm.

"Doreen, it's me. Vince," I said.

She stopped and turned, then took my fingers off her arm. She didn't smile. She didn't seem glad to see me.

"You mean he lets you out alone?" she said. "All by yourself?"

She was sarcastic. All at once I realized that she was jealous. She was jealous of Bentley. I took her hand.

"I've been sitting in the Gigolo for a couple of weeks waiting for you to show up," I said.

"I don't go there any more," she said. "Too many kids and squares and too many college boys trying to pick you up. These places change fast."

"So where do you go?" I asked.

"The Carnivale," she said. "It's creepy but I like it better and the real beats leave me alone."

It was creepy all right, a big place that looked as if it had once been a stable or a garage. The walls were painted dead black. So was the ceiling but from the ceiling they had hung half a dozen fishermen's nets. The waitresses wore black tights and short black tops. On one wall someone had painted a white skull and crossbones. The customers were really beat, no uptown kids or phony college boys but guys and girls who were way out, some of them on pot, just sitting and staring at the fishnets.

They had thirty kinds of coffee and I would have been willing to bet that they also had some very peculiar cigarettes if you were well enough known in the place. We ordered cappucino and sat looking at each other across the postage stamp of a table.

"You were supposed to call me," I said. "You promised to do that when I left. You knew I couldn't call you at the house."

"The Tiger told me not to call you," she said. "In fact he didn't just tell me. He ordered me not to call you. Sugar, you are the private property of Mr. Big and much too good to associate with a little whore lady like Doreen."

"The Tiger doesn't own you," I said. "Bentley doesn't own me."

"Are you kidding?" she said. "Until the day I walk out of the Tiger's house and get into a taxicab and drive to that big white boat, he owns me, all right. And as long as you're living in Bentley's apartment he owns you, sugar. One hundred per cent."

"No," I said, anger rising like an inflamed boil. "I won't sit still for it."

"All right, honey, go and jerk sodas in some lousy drug store," she said. "Walk over to Western Union and tell them you want to start a career in the communications industry. Starting at the bottom. As a messenger boy."

"What about us?" I said. "You and me?"

"About us, nothing," she said bitterly.

I hit the table with my fist.

"No!"

A couple of beats, startled by the sound, looked at us and one of them traced a square in the air with the tip of his finger. Doreen reached across the table and took my hand. When she touched me I tingled.

"Vincent, baby," she said, "you know how it is with me. I'm a whore. I'm not a party girl or a call girl or a business girl or a part-time model looking for the easy dollar. I am a whore that works in a whorehouse. I like it that way. It suits me better because on the outside you can't get along without a personal pimp, a fancy man, and that is one item I've never wanted."

"So?" I said.

"Suppose we both walked out," she said. "I've got some money. So have you. We could spend it up and maybe we'd have a hell of a good time. I don't know. But when it was gone, where would we be? I would still be a whore and you would be a pimp. It wouldn't work out. Forget it."

"There are other ways," I said. "There are other ways of living."

"For us?" she said. "Forget it, Vincent. Put it out of your mind."

We sat in the Carnivale for an hour, talking in the way we had done in the summer before I had moved out of the house. As we talked she brightened up a little. She had missed me too. I could feel that.

We came out of the place into the bright clean sun, blinking after the black walls.

"There aren't any peaches," I told her. "Do you want an apple? A big red apple?"

I bought an apple and we ate it together the way we had eaten the peach. The old Italian pushcart woman had gold rings in her ears, big circles right through the flesh. She laughed at the two of us sharing the apple.

"Thatsa how everything started," she said. "A man, a woman and an apple." She pinched Doreen's cheek. "You gonna be married, huh?" she said. "Easy to see."

She laughed and we walked away. Doreen tossed the core of the apple into the gutter. She stared at it, then said, "A man, a woman and an apple. Where would we all be, I wonder, if Adam hadn't cared for apples?" Then she looked at her watch and said, "Honey, I've got to go. I've got a trick at three o'clock."

It had never bothered me before but now it did. I caught her wrist. I wanted to hold her, to keep her with me.

"I've got to see you," I said. "I'm going nuts. I mean it."

"It's not a good idea," she said. "For you or for me, it's a bad idea. But I'm in that place, the Carnivale, mostly every day."

I kissed her on the cheek and she moved away, her sharp, brand-new heels making a bright sound on the sidewalk. I looked at the watch that was strapped to my wrist. It had been nothing but a piece of jewelry, a lousy ornament. Now it meant something to me. Time meant something to me again. I walked back to Gramercy Park whistling in the street. For the first time in months I felt good. I felt like dancing in the dirty New York street.

After that, every morning at about eleven I went to the Carnivale and sat under the fishnet ceiling waiting for her. Most mornings she came. We would spend an hour together, two hours sometimes. For a long time—three or four weeks—it was almost enough for us just to sit in the coffee house with all the beats in the dark around us, holding hands like a couple of high school kids, just talking about nothing, just being together, away from the Life, away from everything but ourselves.

At the Carnivale it was like being in a cave or perhaps in the hold of a ship. We felt safe in the black room with the candle-light on our faces, queer people all around us, oddballs who had nothing to do with the Life and nothing to do with that other life that went on in office buildings and churches and places like Greenwich and Scarsdale.

I needed her. She needed me. It should have been simple and it was simple.

Too simple.

We had been to bed together as lovers, even if that part of it had only lasted for an hour or two. It had been real for that short pause in time. There was always that between us in both our minds. I wanted to be alone with her and not in some stinking hotel room, even if the room would cost forty dollars a day. I wanted her all to myself in a nice place. A beautiful place. And she wanted the same thing. It was a problem. Neither of us really had the courage to tell the Tiger to go to hell.

Then I got what seemed to me to be the break of my life. At breakfast time Bentley told me that next week they were going to open the play in Hartford for a tryout.

"I want you to come with me, Vincent, but I don't think it's wise," he said. "Hartford isn't New York. It's a strait-laced town full of blown-up insurance salesmen. To be on the safe side, I think I'd better leave you behind."

"How long will you be gone?" I asked, fighting to keep my voice steady.

"Five days, possibly six," he said.

He was casual about it, offhand as if leaving me alone was the most natural thing in the world. During these last weeks his manner had changed. Before he committed himself to the play he had been lifeless and timeless, getting up when he woke up, going to bed when he could no longer stay awake, just drifting with the tide of his life, kept afloat by his money.

Now he was like a businessman, infatuated by activity and movement, always occupied with something that had to do with the play: the sets or the props or the lighting system, the publicity man or the representative of one of the unions. He wanted me there at dinnertime and sometimes he asked me to come to rehearsals with him, but aside from that these last few weeks I hadn't seen him very much. Now for four or five days I was not going to see him at all.

"You'll be all right, Vincent," he said, treating me as if I were a child who had been somehow deprived of a treat. "Jean-Pierre is coming with me. I loathe hotel food, you know. And the two girls will be off. But Daniel will be here to look after you."

"I'll be all right," I said.

My knees were trembling under the table so that the table-cloth fluttered as if it had been caught in a breeze, though it was cool and the windows were closed. I put my hands on my knees and held them still. I knew Bentley. He could change like the evening light. The least hint might make him decide to take me with him, perhaps to keep me locked up in a hotel room for four days. I pretended to be mildly disappointed.

He seemed satisfied. He finished his breakfast and stood up, buttoning his hand-made vest. The suit was smooth gray flannel and he was wearing a tie made of heavy silk the color of dark blood. His shoes were rubbed to a wax finish. Daniel did that with a bone, I knew. His pants were pressed, but not too pressed.

He looked rich, rich as blood, but there was something lacking. I looked at him as he stood in front of the breakfast room mirror adjusting the knot of his blood-colored tie. He was rich and he was successful. He was good at his chosen trade. I knew that from reading the papers, things written about him and the play. In the theater he was no phony. He knew exactly what he was doing and he did it with all the authority of a ship's captain. He was the producer, in command. Everyone touched his cap to Bentley.

But without his money, I thought, he would never have made it, talent or no talent. If he had started in the gutters of life he would never have made it. He was my old man's age or just a few years older. His hands were soft. The old man's hands were like two chunks of hard wood. The old man was a bull, with the strength of a bull. Bentley was a sheep, a soft, rich sheep. The old man could have killed Bentley, snapped his neck the way para-troopers snap the necks of people, or squashed the life out of him with his arms the way you might squash the life from a rabbit. In five seconds, from a standing position, the old man could have killed Bentley.

Then they would take the old man up the river to Sing Sing Prison and strap him into the electric chair and burn the bull life out of him.

But if Bentley had killed somebody, with a knife or a gun or maybe poison, he would not have lost his sheep's life in the chair at Sing Sing. There would have been lawyers and psychiatrists, a dozen of them, two dozen, working to set Bentley free, because that was the way they would earn their pay.

Looking at Bentley in his soft flannel suit I saw the old man for a minute standing there in his T shirt, the stiff strong hair on his chest showing black through the white knit cotton. For a few seconds it was very real. Sharp and real as if I could have reached out and touched the old man's hand. Then it began to fade away like the afterimage of a light when you switch it off or close your eyes tightly.

"Vincent, for the love of heaven wake up!"

It was Bentley's voice, peevish and impatient. I looked up sharply, coming out of my thoughts. It was like coming out of a dream. I blinked for an instant like a man emerging from a dark room and had to force things into focus again.

"Are you in a trance, my dear boy?" Bentley said. "I'm off now to rehearsal. I shall see you at dinner."

I got up. He touched my cheek with the tips of his fingers the way I had touched Doreen's cheek. Don't let him see it, my mind warned me. Don't let him see that he makes you want to puke.

As soon as the door was closed behind him I went into my bathroom and washed my face with soap and water, scrubbing the place where he had touched me, then washing the rest of my face. I looked at myself in the bathroom mirror, then in the bull's-eye that magnified. I moved up close to the little mirror, peering at the pores of my skin. Nothing showed. Nothing. There was no mark of vice on my face. I was just as I had always been, innocent-looking as an altar boy.

"He makes me sick," I said out loud. "He makes me want to vomit."

It was Doreen who had done that. Before I had found her again in the morning on Macdougal Street I had been armored against Bentley. Now when he touched me he made me sick. I wanted to vomit, as if I could somehow vomit the whole thing up, all of my life, and flush it away down the porcelain drain.

I got dressed quickly and walked south to Macdougal Street. It was a spring day, the New York air as clear as water the way it is sometimes, so clear that the edges of buildings and towers stood out sharply against the light and all the colors seemed more intense. Even the people on the streets looked crisper, as if there were new life in them. There was a kind of urban joy that was in the atmosphere itself.

"He's going away on Monday morning," I told Doreen when we were seated at a table in the coffee shop. "Ask the Tiger for a few days off."

"I don't know," she said. "It's not so easy."

She was excited but she was scared too. I could see that. She was afraid of the Tiger's power.

"Tell him it's the time of the month," I said.

She shook her head. "He keeps track of that in a little book," she told me.

"You're not a slave," I said angrily. "Tell him you're sick. Sick at your stomach."

"Sugar, that would be no lie," she said.

I looked at her face in the candlelight. Her skin was pure as milk, just a hint of crimson underglow in her cheeks. Her mouth was firm. Her eyes were dark and intelligent and deep. She was beautiful. I loved her. At that moment in the dark and candle-lighted cave I loved her just for herself and not because I wanted to sleep with her to prove to myself that I was not a dirty little homosexual, but just for herself, for her calm and her beauty, in the way I had loved my mother when I was a child.

She leaned across the table and took my face in her hands and kissed me on the mouth.

"I'll get away, sugar," she said. "I don't know just how, but I'll get away."

I kissed her back.

"Monday morning," I said. "I'll pick you up right here in the Carnivale."

CHAPTER FOURTEEN

O n Monday morning they took off for Hartford, Bentley and
the cook, Jean-Pierre. For five days, Bentley took five pieces
of luggage: three suitcases, a hatbox and a shoebox made of polished leather of the kind that is used for shoes. I watched Daniel
pack for him.

"How will he get all that stuff in the car?" I asked.

"He's going by train with the cast," said Daniel, his flat black
prizefighter's face showing nothing. "You know he's a very demo-
cratic gentleman. He wouldn't want the cast to think he was riding on the high horse."

"Are you kidding?" I said.

"I am a gentleman's gentleman," said Daniel. "I never kid."

Then he winked with his one good eye and I winked back.
He was still a neutral, but I thought that perhaps he could be
turned into a friendly or benevolent neutral, the kind who did
not have to see what went on under his nose. It was important for
him to be friendly because an idea was forming in my mind now,
an idea that burned like a live coal.

I went downstairs and stood on the curb while they got into
the Carey car that would take them to Grand Central. Bentley
got in first. Jean-Pierre touched my stomach with the tip of his
yellow finger the way a cop will touch a person gently with the
tip of his club.

"Watch your step, little boy blue, and keep your *pantalons* buttoned," he said. "The boss does not like to have his personal merchandise handled."

I hated him. He was trying to scare me and I hated him. I could have killed him there on the street, but I kept my face like a choirboy's face and said, "So long, pot walloper, don't get dishpan hands."

The Carey car moved off, rounding the burgeoning little park. It was another bright spring day, clear and beautiful. I felt as though I had just been released from a dark wet prison.

I went upstairs. Daniel was clearing away the breakfast dishes. I took fifty dollars from my wallet, handed him the money and said, "I don't want to eat my meals alone, Danny. I'd rather go out. Why don't you take off as soon as you're finished with the dishes?"

He looked at the money: two twenties and a ten, new money, fresh from the bank, the way Bentley always ordered his money.

"You mean take off for the week?" he said.

I took out another fifty dollars and put the money into his hand.

"That's right," I said. "I won't need you."

"I can't really take off," he said. "But I'll tell you what. I'll come in every morning for a couple of hours by the service door in the back. You won't have to worry about a thing."

"Thanks, Danny," I said. "You're all right."

"I'm a human being," he said. "And I didn't get all my brains knocked out in the ring."

It wasn't the money that persuaded Danny. It was common kindness. That and the chance to help put one over on Bentley, the owner, the grand proprietor, the man whose shoes Danny shined with a bone. I had gambled on Danny and I had won.

He would see nothing and he would not call Bentley's hotel in Hartford to tell Bentley that I had gone off the reservation.

He lifted the tray into the air Pullman-porter style and headed for the kitchen. I went into Bentley's bedroom. I knew that he kept his spare keys in the top drawer of his dresser. They were there, on a gold ring, car keys, house keys, key to the place in East Hampton. I put the key ring into my pocket, then called the garage on the phone that stood on Bentley's night table.

"Will you send Mr. Bentley's car around, please," I said.

I was taking a chance, a long chance. Bentley might have told the garage that he was going away.

"Who is this speaking?" said a voice on the phone.

"This is Mr. Bentley's nephew," I said.

There was a pause, then the voice said, "All right, sir. Five minutes."

I hung up, realizing that I had been a fool to be scared. Bentley was too smart to tell the garage he was going away. If he had done that, by the time he was aboard the train to Hartford some mechanic and his girl friend would already have hit the highway in the Ferrari.

I packed one bag with clothes and a second with liquor, gin, because that was what Doreen liked, and a couple of bottles of brandy. Food we could pick up on the road.

I got behind the wheel of the car, nervous but not scared. I knew how to drive an ordinary car and I had watched Bentley drive this one often enough so that I knew where everything was located. Even so, I wasn't prepared for the feeling of power you get with that kind of engine out in front. You feel it a little as a passenger; driving the car you control it. It wasn't like a machine at all, but more like a powerful animal, a kind of super-super horse, maybe, that did everything you told it to do if you gave the orders in the right way.

I moved out of Gramercy Park and headed for the Village, controlling the urge to step on the gas when I hit the one-way avenue heading downtown. I double-parked in Macdougal Street blocking the traffic behind me. Doreen was there at a little table, a suitcase on the floor beside her.

That means she had made it, I thought. That means she has gotten away from the Tiger.

I picked up the bag. "Come on, baby, we're on our way," I said. "And I am blocking traffic."

Small Italian children crawled all over the Ferrari and traffic behind it was backed up so that a couple of dozen drivers were blasting away on their horns. I tossed Doreen's bag into the car and told the kids to scram. What I didn't want was a cop. I had my phony license but I didn't have Bentley's registration.

"Get in, baby, we're going places," I said to Doreen, holding the door.

The Italian kids screamed and yelled as I moved away from the Carnivale. We pulled through the narrow street. Doreen looked at me, then touched the Circassian walnut panels on the dashboard.

"Sweet Jesus, sugar, did you steal it?" she said.

"I borrowed it," I said, paying attention to my driving as I threaded the car through traffic. I turned north on First Avenue, setting the speed to the automatic lights, and then I relaxed. For some reason I didn't feel like telling lies to Doreen.

"I borrowed it all right," I said. "But I didn't bother to tell Bentley that I was going to borrow it."

"To hell with Bentley," she said very decisively. "There is nobody else but us, sugar. There is nobody else in the whole world."

I cut into the East River Drive and ran the car at about forty, passing only the old jalopies until we had crossed the

Triborough Bridge and were riding on the fast wide parkway. Holding back in that car was like walking a race horse. It didn't seem quite right. Beyond LaGuardia Field I began to open it up a little, to fifty, fifty-five, sixty. I wasn't nervous any more. I had the feel of the Ferrari already and after the first half-hour you would have thought I had been born knowing how to drive it.

"We should have bought some tea at the Carnivale," I said.

Doreen opened her handbag. "Look what mommy's got," she said.

I took my eyes off the road for a second. There were two bundles of reefers, ten cigarettes to the bundle. It was more than we would smoke.

"I've got a suitcase full of booze," I said. "Food we can buy on the way out."

"Who needs food?" she said.

The only thing she had had to drink was a cup of bitter black coffee from the machine at the Carnivale and she had not smoked a reefer, but she was high as a kite. She was way out. She was flying just over the idea of getting away from the Tiger's house and the smell of the Life even for a few days.

At Smithtown we stopped at a grocery store and bought food: bacon and eggs, a dozen frozen steaks, bread and butter.

"Get some beer," Doreen said. "It's a nice thing in the morning instead of orange juice."

The country boy who was waiting on us looked at Doreen as if she were crazy.

"Put in two cases of beer," I told him.

I cut south to the dune road and moved along slowly, looking for the house. There was a blue-and-white enamel sign, BENTLEY, that he had had made to order in France. I couldn't miss it. I turned into the driveway and left the car in the carport where it could be seen from the dune road although there was a garage under the house.

"Anybody passes and sees the car they will think Bentley is here for sure," I said. "Otherwise, if somebody saw us moving around on the beach they might get suspicious and think we had broken into the joint."

I looked at the Ferrari, just twelve cylinders and two seats, the body in a crouch like an animal, the whole thing almost moving even when it was standing still.

"One thing is for sure, you can't miss that car," I said.

"Sugar, you have been developing expensive tastes," said Doreen.

"I love that car," I said. "Just sitting behind the wheel makes me feel like a king. It is the only thing that Bentley's got that I would want."

"Except his money," Doreen said.

"I wouldn't want his money," I said positively. "Not if I had to have what goes with it."

I opened the windows at the side of the house to air the place out. There was the slightly musty smell you get in closed-up places when they are near the ocean, a kind of heavy salt must. Doreen walked out onto the covered deck.

"Good holy Jesus!" she screamed.

I ran out to where she stood.

"What's the matter?" I said. "You sound as if somebody scared you."

She was staring at the ocean, the empty ocean.

"That," she said, pointing at the sea. "Good holy Christ."

I laughed at her. She was nineteen years old and she had never seen the ocean.

"You are a hillbilly peasant," I told her. "In New York even poor people can look at the ocean. Coney Island, Brighton Beach, it's the same damned ocean."

I looked at the long stretch of beach, carpets of pure white sand with nobody on it, and I thought of the beach at Coney Island, lousy with stinking people, so close together they touched one another, the collective stink of their bodies stronger than the clean smell of the ocean.

"It's only the ocean," I said. "But it looks better from here. Take a good look. You'll never get a better view of the sea anywhere in the world than from this deck we are standing on."

Then I remembered that that was something Bentley had said to me when we stood on the deck together, and I was sorry I had said it to Doreen.

"To hell with it," I said. "It's only the ocean. It's only a lot of salt water."

She turned and put her arms around me, then kissed me on the mouth. I moved my hand down her back and pressed myself tightly against her. She backed away.

"Let's wait," she said. "Let's eat and drink and listen to music on the hi-fi and then go to bed together as if we were just ordinary people instead of being what we are."

"What the hell, we are people," I said. "You're a person. I'm a person."

She shook her head.

"We are two whores on a holiday," she said. "But let's pretend we can forget about it."

Sometimes it showed like a raw wound, the vein of bitterness in her, the self-contempt that was in her blood along with the red and white corpuscles that fed her body and kept her alive. It was a thing I did not understand, not that bright afternoon on the beach, but it was something I could recognize in her. It would come to the surface like that, just for an instant. Then it was forced back again to somewhere deep inside her where it festered but did not show.

"I'm hungry," I said. "It's the salt air."

We went into the kitchen. It was fitted out like the kitchen in Bentley's apartment. There were the same copper pots lined to order with stainless steel, the same rack of spice jars or a set just like them, the same row of meat cleavers, each one as sharp as a razor. I took down the ten-inch cleaver and tested the blade with my thumb. I didn't use any pressure but the blade almost went through the tough hide of my thumb. You could see the hairline mark on the skin.

"You should see Bentley's cook handle one of these," I said. "He is an artist with the cleaver."

"A friend of yours?" she said.

"A louse," I said. "A French-Chinese louse."

She took the cleaver out of my hand and put it back on its hook. It quivered on the hook like a struck string, the blade glittering in the light.

"Forget about Bentley," she said. "Blank it out. Just think about you and me and the ocean."

I could feel Bentley standing beside me in his gray flannel suit and his blood-colored tie, touching my cheek, making me want to vomit up my whole dark soul. I sat down on a kitchen chair, watching Doreen move around, trying to shake off Bentley's presence.

Doreen cooked a steak and I made a big pile of toast. The refrigerator had been left on at low speed so there were ice cubes in the trays.

"Do you want a drink?" I said.

"Later," she said. "After lunch I am going to have a swim in the ocean, and I want to be clean cold sober."

"You can't go swimming," I told her. "It's too cold."

"If there was an iceberg right out there I would still go swimming," she said. "Anyway, it's nice and warm."

"In the sun," I told her. "The water is different."

We ate our lunch on the deck, steak and toast and plenty of coffee. The ocean was magnificent. When I had been there with Bentley the water had looked like gray metal. Now it was bright blue in the sun, glittering like blue silk with patches here and there of an intense cold green.

Away off down the beach some people were cooking lunch on the sand. You could see the pale smoke from their fire and there were kids running on the sand, little kids, small as ants from that distance.

The sun was warm but I knew that the ocean would be bitter cold. I had gone in early at Coney Island too many times not to know that. But I also knew that it wouldn't do any good to try to talk Doreen out of going into the water. She was all of a sudden in love with the ocean. You would think that she had discovered it. She was fascinated by it. As soon as we had finished lunch she stood up and began to unbutton her blouse.

"You have to wait," I told her. "After you eat, you have to wait at least half an hour."

"Thirty minutes and no more," she said. "Then I am going into that ocean."

Bentley had a lot of beach property. Several hundred yards to the west stood another big dune house, but the board shutters were up and the beach was deserted. To the east for half a mile were just some closed-up shacks. A long way off was the party on the beach with the little kids the size of ants.

Doreen took off her clothes. I had never seen her body in the sunlight before, but only under electric light or the gray morning light of the city coming into my top-floor room through the slats of the Venetian blinds. I don't think many people can bear the inspection of the full sun. There is not much mercy in sunlight, especially at the beach where the sand picks up the light and intensifies the glare. I had seen them at Coney Island, girls who looked pretty good in the shade, like hags in the bright sun.

Doreen was beautiful. Her skin was gold from the sunlamp and absolutely clear. Her breasts were firm and clean. She was perfect. I knew the way she lived, with the clock turned all the way around, drinking too much gin, smoking marijuana when she felt like it, entertaining an army of guys night after night.

It did not show. There were no marks left by the life of the night. In the raw sunlight on the white primitive beach she looked as healthy and as innocent as anyone I had ever seen.

"Are you coming with me, sugar?" she said.

I pulled off my shirt, then stepped out of my pants and shorts.

"If you're crazy, I'm crazy," I said. "We're together, aren't we?"

We walked across the beach to the water, both of us naked and warm in the sun. The sand under our feet was hot until we reached the part that was wet where the high waves had brushed it. Then it was cold, cold as ice.

"There's only one way and that's to go right straight in," I said. "I know. I've done this before."

I sprinted into the water and made a shallow dive. It was so cold that it felt hot and for the first few seconds I had the sensation of being scalded.

"Come on in, it was your idea," I yelled.

She ran over the wet sand into the surf, running like a frightened chicken, then swam out for a few strokes before the undertow caught her. I saw her head go under and watched for it to come up again. It didn't.

I am a pretty good surf swimmer, if you want to call fighting the surf swimming. I went under the water after Doreen, once, twice, three times. The third time, I found her. I caught her body under the armpits and let the tow carry us out. The minute it slackened off I fought back. In a few seconds, maybe ten seconds, I had Doreen on the dry beach.

She had swallowed a lot of salt water but she was all right. I rubbed her arms, then her legs, trying to rub away the cold. She was freezing cold, shivering in the way you imagine a person would shiver with some kind of tropical fever.

"Don't try to move," I said. "I'll be right back."

I ran up the dune steps and into the house. From the liquor suitcase I took a bottle of French brandy. I opened the bottle and ran back to Doreen. She was still shivering badly, partly from chill and partly from fear. I held the brandy bottle while she drank from it.

"Don't break your teeth on the bottle," I said. "You sound like an adding machine."

She took a slug of brandy, then another, and then lay back on the hot sand, not moving, permitting the rich strong liquor to warm her blood and take the edge from her nerves. I swallowed a mouthful of brandy, then took another, and then stuck the bottle into the sand and lay back beside Doreen.

There was a lot of blue sky and there were no clouds at all, so that the sky looked as if someone had swept it absolutely clean. The blue color was intense.

The brandy and the sun worked fast. In a little while we were warm again. I touched Doreen's hand.

"You might have been drowned," I said. "That undertow is nothing to fool with."

"I know," she said, staring at the enormous sky. "You saved my life."

"I pulled you out, that's all," I said.

"If you hadn't pulled me out I would have drowned," she said. "I didn't know how to get out by myself. So you see, sugar, you saved my life." She sat up, brushing the hair away from her face. "I hope you don't ever regret it," she said. She looked at the ocean. "I hope you don't ever wish you had left me in the water to die and just walked away from everything."

I was looking at the sky, trying to find a cloud somewhere. There wasn't any, not even one of those hazy things you see sometimes, like gauze, high up.

"You can't die," I said. "I need you. I love you."

It was the sky that gave me the words, the high, chalk-blue sky. Her face came down close to mine and she kissed me, holding her mouth against mine. Her mouth was moist and warm and tasted of salt from the sea. Finally she took her mouth away. She stroked my cheek, then brushed back my hair.

"Oh, my baby," she said. "My darling."

It was all new. It was blinding. It had nothing to do with that first night during the summer or even with those other times in the early mornings in my room. It was new in the way the sun is new every time with the fresh dawn. It was the beginning of the world and the end of the world, and there was nothing in the world but the two of us, who had been turned into one.

Then, after a long while, there were the two of us again, together on the long, deserted beach, the warm sand underneath us.

I started to say something. I don't remember what it was. She put her fingers on my mouth.

"Don't talk," she said. "Not now."

She rested close to me so that our bodies were touching. I felt the way I used to feel when I was small and I would wake up in the night and crawl into the bed beside my mother. I was warm and safe and happy.

In the suitcase there were eight bottles of English gin and two bottles of brandy. The only bottle we opened was the one we used on the beach for medicine. We didn't smoke the reefers

Doreen had bought at the Carnivale. She lit one, took a puff, and threw it away. We didn't need anything except ourselves and the beach and the stars at night and the bright sun in the daytime.

It makes you change, to feel that way about somebody else. Nothing makes you change quicker except death, I suppose. I changed all at once as if someone had touched me with a wand. I began to have a conscience again, or something that felt like a conscience.

That night we lay on the beach looking at the stars and at the moonlight on the water, holding hands, not saying much, smoking a cigarette once in a while. My mind drifted in the dark. I could see myself in the dark as if I watched a moving picture of myself, with Bentley, with other people, with old Mrs. Anderson. I was disgusted with what I saw against the black screen of the night, and then I was guilty. I felt the guilt like a rush of blood. There is no other word that describes what I felt as I lay on the beach in the dark night, watching the scarlet calligraphy of our cigarette ends. I was guilty and I was ashamed and perhaps I was sorry for myself. Anyway, I started to cry like a child.

Doreen touched my cheek.

"Help me," I said. "Make it go away."

She made it go away. She held me, with my head on her lap. She stroked my cheek and she sang songs in the night, sweet sad songs she had learned in the South, songs that the colored people sing.

I had the feeling that she had changed in the same way that I had changed.

She was different. I felt that.

When we had been together before, smoking marijuana in my bedroom, we had still been halfway working at the Life. We had talked about the Tiger and the other people who lived in the house, and about tricks we had worked, Mrs. Anderson, Bentley and the others. But underneath us, five stories and basement and cellar, had been the Tiger's house itself so that you could never forget it.

And outside, on that street that ran with a slant and on other streets reaching away for fifty miles in every direction, was the complex of the city, the prison house of New York, the moated city in which I had been born and which I had really never left, to which Doreen had come, not looking for one prison to exchange for another but finding one just the same.

That was the way it had been in the Tiger's house with the city crouching like an animal just outside the windows.

On the Long Island beach with the sheltering dunes behind us and the ocean in front of us, with the white pure sand for a bed, it was almost as if the Life did not exist, had never existed.

The weather held good for three days: bright sun, clear sky, the air warm and clean and dry. I taught Doreen to swim in the surf. We found some charcoal in the kitchen and made a fire in a hole in the sand, a hot clean fire without any smoke. Doreen cooked the steaks over the coals, holding the meat in a wire grill. We didn't see anybody. Once in a while a car would pass on the dune road beneath the house. Far off we could see the family with the little kids. Otherwise we might as well have been on another planet. I was happy. I had no sense of fear.

The fourth day it was cloudy in the morning and after a while it began to rain. We sat on the covered deck watching the ocean. There were big waves a little way out and the surf was running high. It was hard to believe that we had been swimming in the same water a few hours earlier. You could feel the power of the sea, merciless and Greek and impersonal.

Then the wind built up and the rain began to drive in at an angle under the roof of the deck. We went into the house. I was chilly and damp, almost cold. I started to make a fire in the big stone fireplace. Doreen watched me and laughed.

"Sugar, did you ever make a fire before?" she asked.

"Only on the beach or in trash cans on the corner," I said.

"You open some beer and turn on the radio." she said. "Let me fix the fire."

She knew how to build a fire. In a few minutes the place was warm and the flames threw a red light on the slant-roofed ceiling.

"Where did you learn to do that?" I asked. "Build a fire, I mean."

She put on a heavy Southern accent, almost a Negro accent.

"When I was a little girl I lived in a mud-walled cabin," she said. "Only heat we had was the fire, for cooking and to warm the place."

I watched the flames dancing on the logs, scarlet and orange and a sharp chemical green. Then I got up and walked around the room. We hadn't been in the house much, except in the kitchen and to sleep in the big master bedroom. Outside on the beach there had been just the two of us, guarded by the feathery dunes. Here in the house there was Bentley too. Bentley and the Tiger.

I walked around the living room, a beer can in my hand, touching a number of objects with the tips of my fingers: a cigarette box made of soft green stone, a clock with a flat gold face, the set of brass fire tools that stood in a rack on the stone hearth.

"When we leave here I'd like to burn the place down," I said. "I'd like to sit in Bentley's car a little way down the road and watch it burn right to the ground."

"It's insured," she said. "He would only build another house."

"It's not that," I said. "I just don't like the idea of anyone else being here now that we have been here."

About Bentley she was right. I could have burned the house and the car. It wouldn't really have bothered Bentley. It would be just an inconvenience to be solved by writing a series of checks. He might even be delighted; it would give him the excuse to build another house and to order another custom-made car from the commendatore himself.

The only thing that would hurt Bentley would be to know that I had been with Doreen while he was gone. I knew Bentley. That would get him. It would get to him in a way that nothing else would touch him.

I sat down in a deep chair, looking at the fire Doreen had made. I felt sick. I was sick with fear. I was afraid of Bentley, I saw that, just as I had always been afraid of the old man. With the old man it made sense. He was a bull. He could break me in two. But to be afraid of Bentley made no sense at all. Bentley was a fairy, a lousy fairy, and I was a man. I was seventeen, going on eighteen, but I was a man and I knew it.

Still, I was afraid of Bentley and I was afraid of the Tiger and I was afraid of the cook, Jean-Pierre. It seemed to me immoral to be afraid when I was in love. I looked at Doreen. She was relaxed in an easy chair, a beer can on the floor beside her, one leg over the arm of the chair. She looked young and innocent, dressed in shorts and a white shirt.

"Are you afraid of the Tiger?" I asked.

She sat up, tossing her hair.

"You know I am, sugar," she said. "You can make book on that."

We were both afraid. We were objects controlled by other people because we had somehow lost the ability to make decisions for ourselves.

"The Life," I said. "How are we going to get out of it?"

She didn't say anything.

"Why can't we just walk away?" I asked. "Why can't we get up and get dressed and get into that car that is parked outside and start moving, anywhere, just moving until we come to a place where we want to stop?"

"You, maybe," she said. "Not me."

"Why?" I said. "Why?"

"Because for me there is no place to go," she said. "I was born at the end of the line. We could move around the country. We could even move around the world. But it would only be geography. Wherever I went I would still be a nigger."

"Are you crazy?" I said. "You are whiter than I am. What are you talking about?"

"According to the laws of the sovereign State of Alabama, I am a nigger," she said. "And honey, let me tell you, I found it out the hard way."

I didn't believe it. It couldn't be true. I looked at her then said, "It's a lie, Doreen. A dirty rotten lie."

She shook her head.

"I was born in a cabin the way I told you," she said. "My mother was light, the way I am. My father was a little darker. And we were colored. We lived with the colored. Then my father died. He fell into a power saw at the place where he worked. There was a little money that the sawmill gave us. It gave my mother an idea. We went into Montgomery and we passed. For a long time we passed. I went to a white high school. I had almost forgotten that I was colored until two years ago. Then somebody wrote to the school board. They checked my records and moved me to a colored high school.

"I went there just one day.

"I sat in the classroom, black faces all around me, and I couldn't stand it. I walked out of the school and out of the city and I went to bed with the first man who picked me up. Two weeks later I was on my back in a Birmingham whorehouse. When I got the money I came north. I thought it would be different here. I thought I would forget that I was a nigger."

"You are not a nigger," I said.

"Tell that to the State of Alabama," she said.

"Who would know if you didn't tell them?" I said.

"I would know," she said. "I would always know. I would keep on reminding myself inside, every time my heart beat: nigger, nigger, nigger."

"Don't say that any more," I said. "If you say it again I will hit you."

"If you do, use a stick," she said, a thin, hard edge to her voice. "You know what the white folks say where I come from in Alabama? Never hit a nigger with your hand, they say. Always use a stick or a strap."

"I wouldn't hit you," I said.

"No," she said.

We sat staring at the fire. Outside the storm was building up. The high waves shuddered against the deck piles and the thermopane window was wet with spray. All you saw through the sheet of glass was a cut-off section of the storm. It was like a movie close-up of a hurricane. Inside the house we were dry and warm.

"I'm ashamed of myself for being black and then I'm ashamed of being ashamed," Doreen said. "Maybe it would be different if I had grown up really knowing what I was. Maybe then I would want to fight them instead of fighting with myself."

"Don't talk any more," I said.

"All right, honey," she said.

What she had said hung between us in the air like a bomb on a parachute. The room was filled with tension and you could almost feel it filling up, as if someone were injecting gas into the room. I wanted to tell her that it didn't matter. I wanted to help her, to give her my hand. I didn't know what to say or how to say it. It did matter. Not to me but to her. It would have been stupid to try to tell her that it didn't matter. I got up and went to her, sat down on the floor beside her chair.

"We have to go back tomorrow," she said. "I promised the Tiger."

I didn't argue with her. After a while we got up and went into the bedroom. The rain drove hard against the redwood siding of the house, making a tense thrilling sound. We made love in the big bed, then rested on the clean fresh sheets. We changed the sheets every day. It was Doreen's idea. The bed smelled of lavender from the little bags that Bentley's servants had hung in the linen closet.

I lay on the bed with the lavender smell all around me, feeling sick at my heart and in my stomach. It was the Nausea, the French Disease.

"People crack out of jail," I said.

"Not if they build the jails themselves," she said.

She sat up in the bed, her long black hair like a cape on her cream-colored shoulders. She looked straight at the bedposts and when she spoke her voice had a mechanical quality, almost as if she had rehearsed the words.

"I told you in the beginning, Vincent, it is for now," she said. "For this minute, this hour. You think that is changed just because we are here on the ocean instead of in the Tiger's house or in the back of the Carnivale with the beats all around us."

"Something changed," I said. "You know it. Something changed the day I pulled you out of the ocean."

"Nothing changed!" The words came out like bullets. "I told you, Vincent. I was born at the end of the line. From the end of the line there is no place to go. There is only the Life and that is death. Slow death and not very painful, but it is death just the same."

CHAPTER FIFTEEN

THE next day at about noon we closed up the house and left. Before we locked the door behind us we cleaned the place. Unless you had counted the dirty sheets and towels in the laundry hamper, you wouldn't have known that anyone had used the place.

I had wanted to burn it down.

Instead of that I cleaned it up. I even mopped the kitchen floor.

On the road I pushed the Ferrari toward New York at fifty and fifty-five. I was driving it pretty well but it didn't do a thing for me. It wasn't a powerful animal any longer. It was just a machine, an automobile that cost more than others did when you went to the store to buy it. People stared at the car in the way they adways did. It meant nothing. They were idiots, staring at it. I was an idiot, driving it.

All the way into the city we hardly spoke to one another. There was nothing to say. Even the unsaid things were left behind us on the white abandoned beach. After we crossed the Triborough Bridge and floated down the long ramp into Manhattan, Doreen touched my arm.

"You'd better let me out somewhere a long way from the Village," she said. "I'll take a cab to the Tiger's house."

"Whatever you say," I told her.

"Don't get low in your mind," she said. "Just take things as they come, one thing at a time."

I let her out at Park and 68th and put her bag into a cab.

"Good-by, Vincent," she said.

She kissed me on the cheek and climbed into the cab. The gears crashed and the cab moved off.

Just like that, I thought: Good-by. I stood beside the panting Ferrari and watched the taxi move down Park Avenue until it was swallowed up in the traffic. I felt as if the whole world were melting like sick warm wax. She had deserted me, just as my mother had deserted me when she fell on the kitchen floor and died, just as my aunt had deserted me when she took the bull into her bed.

"Doreen," I said. "Doreen."

With her, I thought, I could have taken off, followed my nose to the end of the world if that was where my nose led me, without being scared of anybody. She was my strength. Without her I was a nothing. I was a nobody, able to go nowhere, except to get into the Ferrari and drive it down to Gramercy Park, to call the garage and ask them to come and get the car, and then to sit in the dark enormous apartment waiting for Bentley to come back from Hartford tomorrow or the day after tomorrow.

I got into the Ferrari and drove downtown slowly, holding back. I cruised around Gramercy Park, pulled up in front of the house and parked. The hallman took the bags. I rode up in the elevator and unlocked the door to the apartment.

"Danny!" I yelled. "It's me. I'm back."

There was no answer. I walked into the living room. Bentley sat in his big chair. Beside him on an end table stood a glass and a bottle of twelve-year-old Scotch whisky. He was drunk. I could see it right away. But not gay-drunk in the way he had been on other occasions. He was cold drunk, steel drunk, the way some people are supposed to get on heroin.

"Well, Vincent," he said. "You've been enjoying yourself while your stupid, silly old fool of an uncle was away, *n'est-ce pas?*"

I don't know why I didn't turn around at that moment, why I didn't walk out of the apartment and keep on walking until I came to a place where I wanted to stop. It wasn't fear that held me there, standing at attention like a stupid soldier. It was the sense of dramatic fate; whatever was coming had to come and I was engaged in a role that must be played out until the finish.

"I got bored so I went out," I said. "Is that a crime?"

He laughed at me, then drank from his glass. His eyes were bright from the drink.

"Vincent, you surprise me," he said. "You know that I'm not a stupid person. Why did you assume that I trusted you when I left you here on your own?"

"So I used the, car," I said. "I'm sorry."

He laughed again and drank again, then picked up an envelope from the table, a long narrow envelope such as lawyers use. There were six or seven sheets of paper with typewriting on them, stapled together at the top.

"M—— Investigating Service," Bentley said. "Very reliable people. Trained in the FBI. There is not very much they miss. For example, take the entry for eleven-oh-three on Tuesday. 'Subjects performed an act of sexual intercourse.' And then at eleven-forty-five on Wednesday. 'Subjects performed intercourse.' My dear boy, one usually waits until the sun is over the yardarm, as they say."

He folded the papers and put them back into the envelope.

"My poor, dear boy," he said. "And all that time you didn't know you were performing for an audience. Three men. Around the clock. With high-powered field glasses, I believe."

"All right, I'll leave," I said.

"Shut up, Vincent," Bentley said.

The voice was dangerous. Even the fake fun was gone. He was cruel as a policeman now.

"You will go when I want you to go," he said. He picked up the envelope and slapped it against the edge of the table. "Unless you want to explain these documents to the Tiger. I don't think the Tiger would be very much pleased with you or your little inamorata."

I stood there like a dumb soldier. He was right about that. If the Tiger knew that Doreen had double-crossed him he would be mean, mean enough to beat her to death if that was what he wanted to do.

"You have been a very naughty girl," said Bentley. "And like all naughty girls you must be punished. Take off your clothes, Vincent. All of them."

I knew what was coming and I wanted to run. When I turned, I stopped. There in the doorway was Jean-Pierre, a smile on his round Chinese face.

"I'll kill you," I said. "I will kill you both."

The two of them moved toward me. Bentley was middle-aged and queer, but he was stronger than you would have expected. Jean-Pierre was tough and strong and he knew some Oriental tricks. Against the two of them working together the best street-fighter in the world would not have had a chance. I didn't fight much, but all the time they were working on me stripping the clothes from my body I could feel the time bomb inside of me ticking away, building up pressure. It would have to go off. I knew that. It would have to explode or it would kill me.

Jean-Pierre held me while Bentley tied my hands and feet. Then Bentley got the whip. I was tied to the door frame stark naked.

"You sons of bitches," I yelled. "You bastards."

"You can complain to Inspector D——," said Bentley.

He named a police inspector who came to his parties, a man with three college degrees. I hung there by my wrists, waiting for Bentley to begin. He was right about one thing. I would get nowhere with the police. I was a wrongo. And behind the police there would always be the Tiger. I was alone, undefended. I did not care.

Bentley took his time, testing the long whip in the air, making it snap like a bull whip.

"You are a bad, vicious person and you must be punished," he said in the kind of schoolteacher's voice he used sometimes. He poked me hard between the buttocks, using the handle of the whip.

"Is that what you did with your little whore?" he said. "Like that? Like that?"

The pain was like the pain of a red-hot poker. I bit into my tongue.

"Vicious! Vicious!" Bentley said.

He was self-righteous as a member of the Christian Brothers. He believed that he was right, absolutely right.

The whip whistled in the dead air, then came down on my back. The first few strokes didn't hurt in the way you might expect because the shock of the pain was so intense, but each stroke caused me to catch the breath in my lungs and the pain in my chest was like the stab of a knife. Then I could feel the bite of the whip and feel the blood on my back like warm sweet milk.

Bentley counted each stroke, taking his time between them so that the pain would sink in.

"Eighteen!"

I tried to vomit but it wouldn't come.

"Nineteen!"

There was a sharp bile taste in my mouth.

"And twenty!"

I waited for the next one. It didn't come.

"Go ahead. Kill me," I said, my mouth clotted with stomach bile. "Go ahead. Beat me to death."

"Don't be greedy, Vincent," said Bentley. "Jean-Pierre, *mon vieux,* the iodine."

The iodine on the raw wounds brought me to life a little bit. Then Jean-Pierre cut the rope at my wrists. I fell to the floor, my mouth and nostrils buried in the deep pile of the carpet. Bentley stood over me.

"I hope you have learned your lesson," he said. "The fact is, Vincent, I am very fond of you."

He meant it. Every word of it.

Together they dragged me through the hall to my bedroom. Jean-Pierre cut the rope that tied my ankles. They went out of the room. I heard the key turn in the lock.

I lay on the bed on my stomach, not moving except to breathe: inhale, exhale, in, out, my cheek on the smooth fresh pillowslip. When I finally moved the pain was so intense that I thought I was going to black out. I sat on the edge of the bed, biting into my lip. Bite the bullet. Bite the bullet. The phrase out of some forgotten book went through my mind idiotically like a stuck phonograph record. I got up carefully and crossed the room to my clothes closet. On the floor with my shoes was a bottle of gin that I had put there several weeks ago. I opened it and drank from the bottle, a long drink that made me gag and flooded my nostrils with the medicinal reek of the gin: juniper, glycerine, alcohol, as if somehow the ingredients of the drink had become unblended.

I was groggy with pain but my mind seemed to operate with a new clarity. It was like a computing machine directed to solve a problem in sequence. I had a grim, harsh and Athenian sense of the formalities.

I waited for half an hour before I took another drink. I did not want to get drunk. I wanted enough alcohol in my system to cut the pain to a point where it could be managed by my mind.

The second drink was easier to swallow than the first. By the time I took the third, I could breathe without feeling the sharp edges of the welts on my back.

I looked at my back in the bathroom, using the three-part mirror that was bolted to the door. The strokes all ran in the same direction, diagonally across my back. I wondered vaguely if they would leave scars, then I realized that it didn't matter.

"They will never get a chance to heal," I said to myself. "What difference does it make? Scars or no scars?"

I knew that I had a long time to wait. I put on drawers and a pair of trousers and sat backwards on a straight chair near the window so that I had a view of the park. I could see the English nannies and the expensive baby carriages and the well-dressed old men with flowers in their buttonholes. A cop went by, strolling along, and there were squads of pretty girls in light-colored dresses, coming perhaps from the City College.

I watched it all in the way you will watch a travel short in the movies, half attentive, half not, really waiting for the feature to begin. All of the time I watched the park the important part of my mind was on the floor of the cockroach kitchen where my mother had died. That was what Bentley had done with his whip. He had taken my mind straight back to that day. It was real. It was so real that I could smell the kitchen linoleum and the bug juice that was squirted there by the exterminator's man who went through the building four times a year. I could smell the kitchen through the fumes of the gin. I was there on the floor with the body, but this time I did not lose my faculties, my powers of speech and movement.

Outside the darkness closed in slowly. From that window I could see the sunset behind the buildings on the West Side. The huge sun of cadmium orange was pasted to an airless sky, like the pasted sun on a school child's cutout. The sun moved slowly into eclipse beneath the black teeth of the buildings. It was dusk. The street lights came on and then all around Gramercy Park lights began to show at the windows of apartment houses and private houses and at the big windows of the clubs on the south side of the square.

The key turned in the lock of my door. Quickly I hid the gin bottle under the bed. It was Jean-Pierre with a box of pills in his hand.

"Codeine," he said. "Two of these and two aspirins and you won't feel a thing."

"What is the gag?" I said.

"No gag," said the cook. "Mr. Bentley likes you, St. Vincent. Yes. He is fond of you. He told you that himself."

He put the pills on the night table, then looked at me and laughed.

"I told you to keep your *pantalons* buttoned," he said. "That is one thing Monsieur won't stand for, fooling around with a woman. Even I do not do that any longer."

"How long will he keep me locked up here?" I said, because I knew that the cook would expect me to ask.

"Week, maybe," he said with a shrug. "Ten days. Until he concludes you have regained the possession of your intelligence. A week at least. And do not forget, my little one, there is no way out but down. Fourteen stories."

He went out and locked the door behind him. I switched on my bed light and looked at the little white pills. They were codeine, all right. I had been given them once by a dentist. There were ten pills rolling around at the bottom of the box. I swallowed two and washed them down with a mouthful of gin.

The pills worked fast and they really worked. I felt the pain when I moved. I knew the pain was there. But it didn't matter. And the pills did not make me sleepy. That was the one thing that had worried me. I had to control the pain but I couldn't afford to become groggy or sleepy enough to lose my sense of balance.

Outside in the apartment the hi-fi set came on. There were four speakers in the living room. I could hear the music through my bedroom door: longhair music, Bach, I thought. Then I heard the sound of voices and of high-pitched homosexual laughter. Bentley was giving a party. That meant that I would have to wait even longer than I had thought, perhaps all night long, until dawn showed at the window.

I didn't care. It didn't matter. The IBM machine in my brain clicked over according to plan. I would wait until it was time for me to move, when Bentley was drunk in his bed, asleep.

I sat by the window and waited on the straight-backed chair, using the gin cautiously and at midnight swallowing another pair of codeine pills. I was wide awake and just faintly lightheaded and very clear in my mind, mapping out every move that I was going to make.

At three in the morning by my bedside clock the noise of the party began to slacken off. They were all drunk by now or high as kites on marijuana, sitting around on the floor the way people did at Bentley's parties, giggling in the half-dark.

Soon they would all be gone. Bentley would take his sleeping pills or, if he thought he was too wound up, an injection of Demarol, and he would go into a deep drugged sleep. I knew his habits and I knew the apartment, every corner of it.

I lay on the floor beside the locked door of my room, listening. When there was no sound at all I dressed myself, moving quietly in the dark. The T shirt hurt going over my back but once it was on it felt all right. I put on sneakers and laced them tightly so that they fitted my feet like gloves.

I gave it another half-hour to be sure that Bentley's drugs had worked, then stepped through my bedroom window onto the narrow ledge that ran all the way across the face of the building.

Fourteen stories down was the park, black as pitch, the street lights yellow and moody. The city was quiet, exhausted by the day and night, resting for a few hours now that the bars had closed. The sky was black and full of stars. I was careful but I was not scared. I had put on sneakers with suction soles and they gripped the granite ledge.

I moved across the stone face of the building to the copper downspout which was anchored to the wall. This was the dangerous part. The building was old. If the bolts were loose in the stone I was finished. I wiped the palms of my hands on the seat of my pants, then got a good grip on the copper pipe. I slid down carefully, using my feet on the side of the building.

I stood on the thirteenth-floor ledge catching my breath. A few feet away was the kitchen window, opened six inches top and bottom as it always was when the weather was good. I moved carefully along the ledge and a few seconds later I was in the kitchen.

I stood still, holding my breath. There wasn't a sound. It was as if the whole house had stopped breathing.

I could see the cleavers in the light from the sky, starlight glittering on the steel. I took the big one in my hand and went softly through the pantry, then up the stairs to the top floor. Bentley's bedroom door was open. I didn't waste any time. I did not care whether or not he saw my face in the last seconds of his life.

The cleaver went through his skull. I hit him again and opened his neck. By starlight on the white sheets the blood was black as ink. I did not feel anything personal. It was as though I had been going through a part in a play.

I heard a sound behind me. It was Jean-Pierre, in a gold kimono, half asleep and rubbing his eyes. I was wide awake. I caught him in the throat with the blade of the cleaver, then knelt on the floor beside him and smashed his skull, deliberately, in the way we used to smash turtles with a rock in camp.

All that time the bomb inside me was ticking but it did not go off. I stood there holding my breath until I thought my chest would burst, but still the bomb did not explode. I felt as though I walked through a dream, a sick dream, disorganized, related to what you feel when you are coming out of insulin shock.

The apartment was empty now. I knew that. Daniel, the valet, would be asleep in his basement room. The two maids were asleep in Brooklyn or wherever it was that they lived. I switched on the light. I was not scared or sick to my stomach but I was startled by the quantity of blood. Bentley's bed was soaked with blood and so was the rug under Jean-Pierre's body.

I stood over Bentley, looking down at his pale stomach and at his mutilated sex. Then I put my fingertip into the blood and wrote on the pale wall, random obscenities, the way a kid will write with chalk on the wall of a Yorkville tenement.

I went into Bentley's bathroom and washed the cleaver carefully. Then I took a long, warm shower. The warm water eased the stiffness of the wounds in my back.

Bentley's wallet was on his dressing table. I took the money that was in it: three hundred and twelve dollars. I had no need for the money. I simply took it.

I went to my own room and dressed myself carefully, putting on a new dark suit. I put the sneakers back on. The codeine pills were on the table. I took two, then put the box into my pocket. I picked up the cleaver and tested the blade with my thumb. It was still sharp but there was a nick in the blade, as if I had used it on a chunk of granite instead of on Bentley's skull.

I went into Bentley's office. His sealskin portfolio was on his desk. I zipped it open, threw the papers on the floor, put the cleaver inside and zipped it shut again. I went to the door of Bentley's room and looked at the two of them, dead as rabbits. Then I said out loud: "You dirty homosexual. You dirty little homosexual."

I went down the back stairs and out of the building by the service door, the portfolio under my arm. It was half-past four in the morning. I had plenty of time. I crossed the park and stood on the corner at Fourth Avenue. The empty street yawned widely under the weary lights. In a few minutes, a long way off, I saw the roof lights of a taxi. I stepped out into the vacant street and used the portfolio as a flag. The brakes screeched as the cab slowed down. I climbed in. All I could think of was the night in the summer when I stood on the corner in my chinos with thirty dollars in my pocket and the hack drivers had laughed at me for a jerk kid.

"Eighty-seventh and York," I said to the driver.

The flag went down and the cab moved off, traveling fast up Park Avenue, then through the maze at Grand Central, then zigzagging east. I was full of gin and codeine but my mind was clear and I knew where I was going. I was going home to the neighborhood. I smoked a cigarette, sitting forward in the cab so that my back did not touch the seat.

The cab stopped a block from the house. I paid the driver and got out. The cab moved off in the silent city. It was still dark but toward the East River a little light was beginning to show. The street was empty. The only thing that moved was a cat, prowling on top of the garbage cans.

I walked to the house. There was a passageway that led from the street to the back court. I went through that, recognizing the cellar smell that rose from the scarred brick walls. I went over a board fence and there was the fire escape that led straight to the window of my aunt's room. I will have to do her first, I thought. There was no other way for me to get into the house without waking both of them up.

With my sneakers on, the fire escape was easy. I had done it often as a little kid, times when I had forgotten my key. I took the cleaver out of the portfolio and threw the portfolio away. I tucked the cleaver into my belt. Then I swung up easily and climbed the iron stairs quietly on my rubber soles.

I looked into the room. The bed was empty. It had not been slept in. My heart was pounding. What a fool you are, I thought. I knew where my aunt was and when I thought of it my hand tightened on the handle of the cleaver.

I slipped through the window. The place smelled just the same, of beer and grease and strong yellow soap and the roach stuff the guy sprays from the container that is strapped to his back. Exterminator, I thought. That is me. Vincent Michael Joseph McCaffery, exterminator.

The apartment was pitch black but I knew every dirty corner of it. I had been born in it and for most of my life I had never lived anywhere else.

They were both in my mother's bed. I saw them in the sick light from the window that came from the street lamp down below. I moved in fast, using the cleaver. My aunt was nearest. Just as I struck she turned and screamed. The blade hit her on the shoulder. Then the bull was at my throat.

I fought with him man to man but I could not hold my own with the bull. He got the cleaver and threw it across the room. Then he pinned me to the floor with his big bull knee on my chest. I felt the pain in my back. Then I heard the sound of my aunt's screaming.

Let him kill me, my mind was saying. Let him kill me with his big knee, squeezing the life's breath out of me.

People were breaking in the door.

"For the love of God, what's going on?"

It was Mrs. Mulleady from 2B. I had known that voice since the day I was born: a high, thin Antrim brogue. The bull was on top of me. I felt his weight shift a little.

"You had better call the police," he said. "Tell them it is an emergency."

The old man held me on the floor until the cops came. They put the handcuffs on me. I began to scream. One of the cops slapped my face. The other one was fixing my aunt's shoulder. I saw the ring on her finger, plain gold like my mother's ring.

"My back!" I screamed. "My back is bleeding."

They took the handcuffs off my wrists and stripped off my coat and shirt. My back was bleeding. It was the truth. I could feel it, warm and wet. The old man looked at the marks of the lash.

"For God's sake, Vincent, who did that to you?" he said.

"You did," I said. "You did it."

The cops looked at my back and then they looked at the old man.

"Mister, that's against the law," one of them said.

"I never did that," the old man said. "He is my son, may God forgive me, but I never put a hand on him but once in my life and that was different."

"You did it," I said.

"I think the kid is psycho," said one of the cops.

"Let's take him in," the other one said.

All the way to the station house and all the way downtown, I forgot about Bentley and Bentley's cook lying on the floor of Bentley's bedroom. Then I remembered and I told them. They didn't believe me.

"Psycho kid," one cop said.

"It's true," I said. "Go and look for yourself."

At Bellevue, in the prison yard, they put bandages on my back and shot my arm full of morphine.

"A mainliner," I said when the doctor put the needle into my arm. "Now I am a mainliner for sure."

There were bars at the windows and there was a cop on a chair beside my bed.

"Do you think he's psycho, doc?" said the cop.

"Who knows?" the doctor said.

The morphine was beginning to work. I was flying and I didn't want to fly. It was the bull. If he lived to be ninety years old I would never be able to beat the bull. There was no sense in living, but as the morphine spread through me, making me fly, I knew they would make me go on living, like this, behind bars.

All my life I had been in a prison: the prison house of my mother's love, the old man's apartment, after she died, the God damned military school, Bentley's apartment, the Tiger's house ... they had all been prisons in their way and now I was in another kind, with real bars at the windows and a live cop on the chair beside me.

"If the kid isn't psycho he's awful smart," the cop said reflectively, swinging his club. "Suppose he had just killed the faggot. He would be a cinch for Murder One. But killing the Chink and then trying to kill his old man and his stepmother, he is a setup for a psycho plea. I'll give you ten to one, doc, that he never even comes to trial."

The words were there in my mind but the morphine did not permit me to say them.

"Let me die," my mind repeated. "Kill me. Let me die."

The morphine was putting me under. I was flying without any engines. Outside there was the city with its common pulse quickening as it rolled through the day, speeding up, racing, as it longed for the night.

CHAPTER SIXTEEN

Six years.

A year of silence and electric shock, of insulin and the naked walls, and then five years in which I have been quiet and safe and happy. I am here safe with my friend and the private world of my own creation.

I do not want to leave this place. My courage fails. But of course Dorion is right. He knows. He is almost the oldest inhabitant. Soon they will arrange that I ask to leave, to go out beyond the armed walls, to stand before a judge and hear the indictment for murder dismissed.

They send for me this morning. I have washed my hands but new earth from the fields of the farm clings stubbornly under my nails. My hands are workman's hands, the hands of a farmer.

The doctors tell me something.

My father is dead. He has fallen from the scantlings high above the street and he is dead. From the high scaffold he has fallen.

"Two years ago. Not quite," they say.

They would not tell me this, I know, unless it was time for me to go. Dorion was right. I lean forward in the straight chair.

"You tell me now?" I say.

"Yes," they say. "We tell you now."

He is dead. I sit in the chair. The old man is dead. Through the blur of the tears I see him, strong as an Irish bull and brave. I weep now and the tears fall like salt rain for my father and myself.